THROWN TO THE WEREWOLVES

A WILDWOOD WITCH MYSTERY: BOOK 5

ELLE ADAMS

1

———

For the Head Witch, even an event as mundane as a flower contest could turn into a life-or-death situation. Not because of witchy assassins or deadly magical monsters but because nothing drew out my family's rivalries quite like a good old-fashioned competition, even one that didn't involve magic at all.

That didn't mean it was harmless, of course. Flowers were serious business.

Tansy, my squirrel familiar, hopped onto my shoulder to get a better view as my mother faced off against her younger sister, blocking Aunt Shannon from accessing a stack of the boxes that covered the damp grass of the field. They both already had their wands out, which only increased my concern that the pair would start an actual duel over who got to set the stage for the flower contest at the town's annual midsummer festival.

Just another day in the life of a reluctant Head Witch.

"Put your wand down and step away from there at once," Mum ordered. Unlike me, she had the sort of booming voice that commanded authority and made me want to take a step back even when I wasn't on the receiving end. "I'm perfectly capable of putting up a tent by myself, and I'll thank you not to interfere."

"I simply thought you might want a hand," my aunt said in innocent tones. "This is a large undertaking, after all."

I didn't buy her feigned concern for an instant. My aunt rarely offered to help unless she thought she had something to gain. While she and my mother were almost identical in looks, tall and lean with blond hair—though my mother's was loose and flowing where her sister's was tied back below a pointed hat—the similarities ended there. Aside from their mutual desire to win, they couldn't have been more different in their approaches.

"It's the same as it is every year." Mum gave a flick of her wand, and one of the cardboard boxes flew open. Red fabric swirled out while wooden pegs flew into place, and in no time at all, a large tent covered a sizeable portion of the field designated as the site of the summer carnival.

"Wouldn't it save time if I helped?" Undeterred, Aunt Shannon made for a nearby pile of unopened boxes.

"If you want to help, I'm sure the shifters would be grateful for your assistance in setting up the snack tables," Mum said. "I'll handle this myself."

Aunt Shannon scowled, but Mum ignored her. With another flick of her wand, colourful banners unfurled and draped over the outside of the tent. The flower contest had once been a modest annual event held at the town hall, but in typical Wildwood fashion, my family had decided to make it into a massive fete that drew attention from every other magical town in the region. As a result, most people who attended the carnival wouldn't even care about the results of the flower contest. Market stalls filled the field, the local werewolf pack had set up vans to sell freshly baked goods, and there was a play area for the children, complete with a set of model unicorns to ride on.

Every year, the theme was slightly different—on one memorable occasion, someone had even set up a miniature ghost train that would run through part of the forest in the evenings—and since this was the first time in months Wildwood Heath would open its doors to the rest of the magical world, I had no doubt Mum had more surprises in the works. Pity the sour look on Aunt Shannon's face was enough to send even the most enthusiastic carnival-goer fleeing in the opposite direction.

"What is it?" Mum finished draping flower-patterned curtains over the tent's entryway and spied her sister still lurking nearby. "If you want to discuss the timing of the contest, take it up with the rest of the council, not me."

That's still bothering her? The subject of which day to host the contest had occupied the past three coven meetings, to the extent that I'd had to put my foot down and remind them that we had other concerns to discuss as well, such as security. Personally, I didn't object to getting a free day off in the middle of the workweek, even if I had to spend it watching my mother win yet another prize for her admittedly spectacular collection of roses. Though I had to wonder why she'd dragged me out here on a Saturday morning to help set up the carnival but seemed to have no intention of letting me actually do anything. I'd much rather have slept in than watch her bicker with my aunt.

"Don't we have more important concerns?" Aunt Shannon enquired. "If you ask me, we ought to have devoted more of our focus to matters of security. You had a narrow escape from a dangerous killer recently, didn't you?"

Mum narrowed her eyes at her sister. "That's irrelevant. We weren't the targets."

Not that time, I wanted to add, but I didn't need to give my aunt any more fuel for her argument, especially as she'd stolen the point from my own irritable comments at yesterday's coven meeting to begin with. I didn't for a minute believe she was genuinely concerned for anyone's safety except for her own, especially as my fellow Head Witches had been the targets of the serial killer in question. I'd likely been spared because I hadn't made quite as many enemies as some, but it had been yet another an unwelcome reminder of how many people saw the sceptre I carried as a challenge.

"I disagree," said Aunt Shannon. "We wouldn't want to lose another Head Witch in such a short space of time, would we?"

From her perch on my shoulder, Tansy made a sceptical noise. "As if she wouldn't have been first in line to snatch the sceptre."

"Don't give her ideas," I said in an undertone. "I bet she was disappointed when she found out I survived."

My aunt hadn't even been invited to the meeting, but the entire magical world was aware of my involvement thanks to the press, which had decided to plaster my face all over every article about the Head Witch meeting that had ended in two deaths. Hardly fair if you asked me.

Aunt Shannon evidently disagreed—unless she was scrambling for an excuse to push my mother out of organising the carnival so she could rearrange the event according to her own whims, which was entirely possible.

"The coven is more than prepared for any future threats," Mum informed her sister. "Now, kindly get out from under my feet."

"I think there's plenty of room for all of us." Aunt Shannon turned her back and sauntered away.

Honestly. A summer carnival was supposed to be a bit of light relief for everyone, but Aunt Shannon was never able to resist the opportunity to undermine her sister's authority as head of the coven.

When my aunt disappeared into the tent, Mum didn't hesitate for an instant before following her. Sensing danger, I followed and entered the tent in time to see my aunt conjure up a large wooden stage with a flick of her wand.

"Stop that at once!" Mum commanded. "I won't have you sabotaging all my hard work."

"I'm not sabotaging anything," said Aunt Shannon. "I thought we could use somewhere for the judges to stand— and the winners, of course, too."

"Where exactly did you get that stage?" Mum asked. "It looks like the one from the town hall."

"They won't miss it for a couple of days, will they?"

"Yes, they certainly will." Mum raised her wand. "If you don't put it back, I'll do it myself."

"This is unnecessary," said Aunt Shannon. "Really, Roxanne, I didn't realise you were so insecure about your own status."

"Insecure?" Mum echoed. "The mayor will hardly appreciate us stealing his property from underneath his nose."

"I seem to remember that it technically counts as our coven's property."

Tansy's fluffy tail tickled my ear. "Let's leave them to it. It's safer that way."

"I'm not so sure." The tent was flimsy enough that one miscast spell might set it on fire, and my mother and aunt were a danger to one another unless they were as far from each other as possible. Like, on opposite sides of town.

Mum pointed her wand at the stage, which vanished in a flash. "If you want to bring a stage, you can buy your own."

"Or I can ask the mayor myself. I'm sure he'll understand." In another flick of Aunt Shannon's wand, the stage reappeared in the same place as before. Oh boy.

"Mum, Aunt Shannon, cut that out," I said, but they both ignored me.

With a flourish, they pointed their wands directly at each other instead of at the stage.

"Fight, fight!" Tansy reared up on my shoulder in excitement.

"Hey!" Striding forward, I inserted myself between Mum and Aunt Shannon with my sceptre at the ready. I didn't plan to use it, but it lessened my chances of being turned into a walnut. "This is a ridiculous reason to start a public duel. There's no reason you can't send the stage back and *then* ask the mayor for permission to borrow it, is there?"

"Head Witch, I'd kindly ask you to stay out of this," said Mum.

"It's none of your business," added Aunt Shannon.

"It's my business if you two blow each other up," I informed her. "Which is possible, given that there's a massive box of fireworks right outside this tent. Besides, I bet everyone else in the field can hear every word of your bickering."

Not necessarily true, but it was strange to be the one lecturing my mother and not the other way around. While I hadn't got into trouble for starting a fight since my days at the local witch academy, Mum was forever reminding me of how every one of my actions reflected on the coven and on Wildwood Heath as a whole, whether I liked it or not.

"What is going on?" The voice came from the tent opening, and my brother, Ramsey, stuck his head inside. Naturally, I was the first target of his disapproving stare, though I lowered my sceptre and did my best to project an air of *Don't look at me.*

Mum and Aunt Shannon stepped away from one another while my brother ducked into the tent properly, as impeccably dressed as usual with his blond hair combed flat against his head. His hedgehog familiar, Prickles, sat on his shoulder, a stern expression on his little face that mirrored his owner's.

"There you are, Ramsey," said Mum. "Your aunt and I were having a discussion about the merits of bringing a stage into the tent for the judges to use."

"I didn't know you needed your wands for that." He directed that comment towards Aunt Shannon as if he'd guessed immediately who the culprit had been.

"Your aunt and I had a mild disagreement over whether it would be apt to ask the mayor for permission before borrowing his property." Mum flicked her wand in a graceful motion that once again banished the stage from sight. "Or if it would be more appropriate to find our own."

"The latter, I would hope." Ramsey eyed the spot where the stage had been.

"They were fighting," Tansy said unnecessarily. "Another minute, and the tent would have blown sky-high."

"Don't be absurd." Aunt Shannon put her wand away and strode towards the tent opening. "I will speak to the mayor myself if it truly concerns you so much."

As she departed, Mum faced my older brother. It surprised me a little to see him here; as the head of Wildwood Heath's small police force, he surely had more important things to do with his time than to break up duels between family members who ought to know better.

"To be clear, she's acting without my approval," Mum told him. "Whether the mayor says yes or not."

"I thought as much," Ramsey said.

"Is it not worth letting her have this one?" I asked. "It's not a bad idea to have a stage set up for the judges rather than everyone standing on the floor."

Mum levelled a glare at me. "This isn't an isolated incident. Give her any leverage, and she'll push for more."

"Is there a way you can reach a compromise with her?"

"No," she said bluntly as if I'd suggested taking up skydiving. "If I give her a twig, she'll take the whole broomstick."

Honestly. She'd been more willing to negotiate when we'd both thought my aunt had tried to have me assassinated.

"I don't disagree, but it's not like you're letting her take over anything important, like hosting other Head Witches..." When her nostrils flared in warning, I added, "You can always tell the other coven members and make it sound as if getting a stage was your idea, not hers."

"And how exactly do you propose I do that?" she enquired.

"People will believe you, won't they?" While I was Head Witch, Mum was still the leader of our coven, and my aunt had a death wish if she thought my mother would lie down and let her undermine her authority. "The rest of the council won't be any the wiser. *I* can tell them if you like."

Ramsey lifted a brow. "Robin, are you offering to go back to work on a Saturday?"

"What do you think I'm doing right now?" I frowned at him. "And no, I'm not. I have other plans this afternoon. I was just making a suggestion."

"I can guarantee she'll find a way to tell the entire coven herself by tomorrow," said Mum. "I realise you think this is a trivial matter, Robin, but this is the first time we've opened up the town to the public since the unfortunate incident a few weeks ago."

As if I could forget it. The incident in question had left one person dead, another hospitalised, and the leader of our main rival coven in jail for attempted murder and the use of illegal magic in an attempt to undermine our coven's authority. Not to mention the authority of the Head Witches as a whole. After Aunt Shannon had turned out *not* to be involved in that debacle, I thought the two of them had turned a corner, but apparently not.

"It's certainly not trivial," said Ramsey. "With that being said, security is going to be tight throughout the event, and I doubt your sister will want to ruin the coven's reputation in front of outsiders. She won't try anything too drastic, I'm sure."

"She certainly won't." Leaving the spot where the stage had been, Mum made for the tent's opening. "I'll tell the rest of the council myself. I need to stop at the house and have a word with Piper."

She ducked outside, and my brother and I left the tent a moment later.

"What're you doing out here, anyway?" I asked Ramsey. "Not dropping in to see Dad?"

"No," he said stiffly.

That figured. Our dad's cottage was only a short distance away from the field, but Ramsey had been much slower to forgive Dad for our parents' separation when we were kids. Never mind that Dad had drawn the short straw since he hadn't had Mum's connections or family reputation to shield himself from the press, and the fact that he'd since remarried a shifter was just another strike against him.

Personally, I thought Jessica and her two kids were awesome and that Ramsey was missing out by refusing to speak to them, but I'd lost that battle enough times already, and it wasn't worth the energy of revisiting the subject yet again. Ramsey would have to make the decision on his own.

"Then what?" I fell into step with him, and we walked past stacks of boxes and half-assembled stalls and tents.

As a warm breeze ruffled the trees around us, he irritably tried to flatten his blond curls with one hand. "I'm here to check up on the security measures, as I said. My officers are setting wards to detect any hostile magic in the area."

Sure enough, I spotted several other uniformed officers near the woodland path. The witches and wizards among their number held wands in their hands—more of the latter than the former, because the majority of the town's witches worked for the coven, not the police.

"Did you bring every single officer over here?" I asked. "Isn't there anyone left at the police station?"

"They can manage without us for an hour, can't they?"

If you asked me, that was just asking for trouble, but I knew better than to think my word held any weight. Mum had already left the field and headed down the trail that led through the woods towards home, so I parted ways with my brother and followed.

My mother was quick on her feet when she wanted to be; I saw no signs of her as Tansy and I walked home—or rather, to the house that I now found myself reluctantly living in for the first time since I'd left home at eighteen. At three stories tall and equally wide, the house was entirely too big for three people to live in, but my family never did things by half measures.

I entered via the back gate and made my way through the vast garden while Tansy ran to the bird feeder to harass the local pigeons and blackbirds. After passing several rows of neat flower beds, I found Piper carefully pruning Mum's prize-winning roses. Her long black hair was tied back, and mud stained her pale hands to the elbows.

"Back already?" she asked. "Is the contest tent already set up?"

"Not entirely," I said. "My aunt decided to step in and 'borrow' the stage from the town hall without asking the mayor."

"She didn't, did she?" Piper snorted. "There's nothing she won't do for attention, is there?"

"Or to get under Mum's skin. The annoying thing is that it worked."

"They didn't start fighting, did they?"

"Almost," I said. "Ramsey showed up before things got too heated."

"Lucky." She clipped another rose. "She has me putting protective spells on the garden every night to stop your aunt from getting in. Are you sure she's not a little paranoid?"

"It's not unwarranted," I said. "Imagine the furore if her flowers ended up damaged and Aunt Shannon won the contest instead! We'd never hear the end of it."

"I guess not, but all the security around the carnival is supposed to be directed more at threats from outside town, not on the inside, right?"

"Pretty much."

We couldn't close ourselves off from the rest of the magical world forever, but the unfortunate truth was that entirely too many people wanted me removed from my position as Head Witch. While we'd taken out one major obstacle when we'd jailed Tiffany Henbane, other potential threats remained, such as the other regions' witches who'd lost the chance to become Head Witch when I'd taken the title. My long absence from home had left me with little chance to prepare for my new position, and while I was learning as fast as humanly possible, a new complication seemed to arise every day.

For instance, I'd discovered another potential collection of enemies whose sole aim was to bring down the Head Witches as a collective. The fact that I'd been chosen by the sceptre against my will didn't seem to matter to those people either.

The glass doors at the back of the house opened, and Mum emerged into the garden. "Robin, I thought you were going to speak to the rest of the council."

"I never said that." Hadn't I told her I had plans?

"I'm sure your lunch date with that Harvey can wait for another time."

"It's not a lunch date. I'm meeting Dad for coffee."

My words predictably slammed a lid on her comments. "I see. In that case, I will contact them myself."

When she about-faced and re-entered the house, Piper and I exchanged raised eyebrows. Bringing up my dad was the one surefire way to win an argument with Mum, and while I didn't technically need to head to the café for another hour or so, calling every council member would take much longer than that.

Being able to see my dad was one of the few perks of being stuck in my childhood home again, though I didn't get to visit him as often as I'd have liked. The other perk was Harvey, my former crush, though our relationship was moving slower than I'd have preferred thanks to our busy schedules. We'd gone out to dinner last night, but I'd arrived back at the house to the unwelcome news that I'd be expected to help at the carnival today. I drew the line at skipping out on spending some quality time with the one family member who didn't expect anything from me, though.

Well, two family members, since my cousin Rowan worked at the same coffee shop where I'd be meeting Dad. She'd settled into her new position well after the upheaval of being estranged from her close family, though being away from Aunt Shannon, her mother, could only have been an improvement. That didn't mean my aunt had forgiven her for leaving the coven, however.

Aunt Shannon carried grudges like nobody's business, and I had little doubt that we hadn't heard the end of her argument with Mum yet.

2

I arrived at Were's My Coffee? shortly before I was due to meet my dad, and the pleasant smell of coffee and baked goods enveloped me as I entered the cosy were-wolf-run establishment. My cousin Rowan waved at me from behind the counter, where she was attending to a long line of customers. As it was lunchtime on a Saturday, the place was packed, and there were no tables available. I waited for my dad near the door, somewhat hindered by the group of teenagers crowding the doorway, drinking smoothies and exchanging gossip. After one of them almost trod on Tansy's tail, she scampered outside to chase some pigeons instead of waiting inside.

I scanned the tables to see who might be getting ready to leave and saw that one window table was unoccupied, but someone had swiped all the chairs. The noise emanating from the central table revealed the culprits; anyone who tried to cross the middle of the café had to step around a group of elderly witches who'd grabbed every nearby chair to form a huddle around their table.

As I moved closer, curious as to what kind of meeting

they were holding, a seventy-something woman in a bottle-blond wig flagged down a nearby barista. Rowan's co-worker, a weedy-looking shifter, shuffled gingerly over to their table, balancing a tray of drinks in each hand.

"Come on, give me my iced tea." The elderly witch snapped her fingers. "Get a move on."

How pleasant. Mumbling an apology, the poor guy shuffled forward to hand out the drinks to the waiting witches. Most of them didn't thank him, continuing their discussion as if he wasn't there.

"I assume you're all ready for the contest?" the blond-wigged woman asked her companions. "I happen to think we're in with a real chance of ousting those Wildwood witches from the winning position this year. My rhododendrons are positively blooming. They'll put the coven's to shame."

They were entering the flower contest? If they thought they could outdo my mother's roses, they'd be sorely disappointed, but I didn't feel strongly enough on the subject to wade into the middle of that argument. Better to let them find out the hard way.

"I'm sure you've guessed that Monday's meeting is cancelled," the blond woman went on. "To give us all time to prepare for the contest."

"Cancelled?" one of the witches said in shocked tones. "No... that can't be. I needed to ask for your advice on my peonies."

"Our next meeting will proceed as planned, but since the coven decided to host the contest on a Tuesday, I need the night off. I'd wager some of the rest of you do too."

The witch sitting on her left, who wore daisies intertwined with her grey curls, chuckled under her breath. "Yes, it'll be quite the show."

The blond witch climbed to her feet, her chair scraping the wooden floor. "I'm going to powder my nose. I'll be right back."

She ambled away from the table, knocking her neighbouring witches' chairs to either side in the process.

When she'd gone, the daisy-haired witch gave another chuckle. "Have any of you heard the rumours?"

"Heard what?" asked the witch who'd expressed such dismay at the cancelled meeting.

"A little bird told me the coven has recently acquired a quantity of thorn-killer toxin," replied the daisy-haired witch. "It's heavily toxic to plants, you know."

"The Wildwood Coven?" echoed the witch. "Why? You don't think they plan to use it to manipulate the contest?"

"They can't." Daisy Hair gave another titter. "Because I took it from them."

"You didn't," said a witch with a straw hat perched on her head. "Did you?"

"Yes, I did." The witch moved in her seat, her foot nudging a flowery handbag that sat underneath her chair. "I might not *need* to use it, but it would level the playing field a little, wouldn't it?"

What are they talking about? Mum certainly hadn't mentioned the coven obtaining any plant-killing toxins, but she didn't need to cheat her way to victory. I inched closer to their table but realised too late that with the blond witch gone, the others had full view of my sceptre if they looked in my direction. Hastily, I ducked behind a pair of burly shifters who sat at the table next to the witches', paying no attention to anyone around them. Then I tuned back in to the witches' conversation and stiffened when I caught the words "Head Witch."

"Isn't she that failure of a grandchild whom the former

Head Witch sent away from town to get rid of her?" asked the straw-hatted witch.

Heat rushed to my face, and my hands curled into fists. Her comment wasn't even true, but I resisted the impulse to contradict her. Losing my temper in a packed café would not help my desire to avoid unnecessary attention.

"That's the one," said Daisy Hair. "No, we don't need to worry about *her*. She didn't inherit Willow *or* Roxanne's gift for flower spells. Or the other sort of spelling, from what I recall."

"That was her?" The straw-hatted witch cackled. "I assume she'll be keeping her distance."

My flush deepened at the intrusion of an unpleasant memory. Back when my grandmother had been in charge of organising the flower contest herself, she'd liked to strong-arm the coven's apprentices and academy students into helping with the setup. One year, she'd volunteered me to create a banner introducing all the contenders, and I'd accidentally written "flower club" as "flour cub." Evidently, the club's members remembered the incident as clearly as I did.

I didn't need to humiliate myself even further by revealing I could hear every word they said, but if Daisy Hair was telling the truth about stealing from the coven, I was pretty sure my mother would want to know.

A faint purple glow drew my attention to my sceptre reacting to my anger, so I stowed it behind my back and forced myself to listen to the two shifters at the nearby table instead while I got my temper under control.

"Really, I'm not surprised I was picked for the promotion," one of the shifters was saying. "I went out of my way to prove my worth to the company. I'm not saying you *didn't*, but..."

His companion grunted, his elbows resting on the table.

Taking that as encouragement, his friend continued. "I'm sure they'll promote you, too, if you work hard enough..."

Another grunt.

This wasn't nearly an interesting enough diversion to keep me from tuning back into the witches' conversation, but luckily, my dad entered the café at that moment, capturing my attention. Short and chubby with thinning dark hair, my dad was positively ordinary-looking compared to the other side of my family.

"Robin." He beamed and wrapped me in a hug. "Are there any tables free?"

"One, but no chairs." I led him to the table in the window and gestured in the general direction of the flower club witches. "Unless we swipe one from them. They don't seem to like me much."

He glanced towards the elderly witches. "Want me to have a word with them?"

"Definitely not." My mother would have picked a fight regardless of what I asked, but I trusted Dad not to go against my wishes. "How's your day been so far?"

"Good," he replied. "How about you?"

"I've had better." I gave him a brief summary of Mum and Aunt Shannon's argument over the flower-contest tent. "I'm supposed to have the weekends off, and honestly, I don't know why she wanted me there. Ramsey was the one who managed to break up the fight between the two of them, so I feel like I might as well have stayed at home."

"Your brother's still doing well, then?"

"Still overworking and proud of it, if that's what you mean."

"Some things never change."

Rowan approached our table, having managed to extricate herself from the endless line of customers. "Should I take your order while you wait for another table? I'll let you know if I see any free chairs."

"Cheers. Get me the usual."

"I'll have the same," said Dad. "It's good to see you, Rowan."

"Same to you." She swivelled to face me. "Do I hear my mum's been up to her old tricks again?"

"Yeah, and now it looks as if I'm going to have to report certain people for cheating in the flower contest before it even gets off the ground."

Rowan followed my gaze to the table of elderly witches. "Cheating? Really?"

"They're claiming to have swiped some kind of plant-killing toxin from the coven. First I've heard of it."

Her lips pursed. "Weird. I can have a snoop..."

"You don't have to." Unlike me, Rowan wasn't obligated to play an active part in our coven anymore, and she was thriving here, making coffees instead of living in fear of angering her controlling mother.

Aunt Shannon hadn't been responsible for acquiring this so-called toxin, had she? If anyone would be duplicitous enough to try to cheat in the flower contest, she certainly fit the bill, but it was possible Daisy Hair was lying or exaggerating. I didn't know her or the others well enough to make a judgement call.

"It's no big deal," Rowan said. "Granted, I don't have as much free time on my hands these days."

"Neither does your mother, so I don't know why she's chosen to occupy her attention with micromanaging the carnival," I said. "Or why *my* mother is making such a big deal of it. Unless she thinks her sister's going to try something at the contest..."

"She probably is," said Rowan. "It's the first time the town's opened to outsiders since... you know."

"Since the assassination attempts," I finished. "We don't have to dance around the subject."

"In public, we probably should," said Rowan. "I tend to avoid talking about the coven here. It took a while for my new co-workers to figure out who I was, and it was honestly kind of nice when they didn't know."

"How did they not realise?" Rowan's short, spiky pink hair and bright clothing set her apart from her mother, admittedly, but the Wildwood name alone should have been enough of a clue.

Rowan's cheeks went pink. "Well... I did put my dad's surname on my application. My boss knew from the start, though. It's no secret."

"Oh." Her dad, Aunt Shannon's ex-husband, had died a few years ago, and it was common coven gossip that my aunt had had him bumped off. I had to admit it was entirely possible, and so did Rowan herself. Her dad hadn't really been involved in her life, but she'd exiled herself from the coven already, so I didn't blame her for shedding the Wild-wood name.

"I thought Richie was going to quit in protest when he found out," she added, referring to her fellow barista. "He was very proud of the staff being comprised of shifters only before I came along."

"Weird attitude for a shifter," my dad commented. "In my experience, they're more welcoming than the covens are... no offence."

I poked him in the arm. "Come on, we both know that's not offensive; it's true. The coven couldn't be less welcoming if they threw visitors into a pit of snakes."

Rowan snorted. "Yeah, well, some shifters want as little

to do with the coven as possible. I'm lucky my boss gave me this chance."

No kidding. Her boss, Mal, was also her landlord, as she lived in the flat above the café. I spent more time in there than my own room, as we'd made a new tradition of hanging out at her place, playing video games at the weekends whenever I didn't have a date with Harvey.

"He's a good sort, Mal is," said Dad.

"You know him?" Rowan asked.

"He knows all the pack shifters," I said. "He's married to one, remember?"

"I don't know *all* the pack," he said. "Like I said, some are anti-coven, and my own history is an awkward subject at gatherings."

Meaning his marriage to my mother. Come to think of it, one of his kids becoming Head Witch might have resulted in some tension within the pack as well. My dad was not a complainer at all, so I often forgot that the coven's antics impacted him as well and the pack by extension.

"If any of them gives you any trouble, you can introduce them to me," I said. "I joke. My mother would throw a fit if I got into a fight with a werewolf."

"Solving their problems by duelling or brawling is pretty normal for the shifters," Dad said mildly. "Personally, I think it's an improvement in some ways."

"As opposed to arguing across a table in a meeting room and talking in circles?" I snorted. "True. I think I'd sooner have watched the council fight a duel to make a decision on which day to hold the contest than listen to them argue for hours."

"What does it matter what day the contest is?" Rowan wanted to know.

"Seems to be an issue for some," I said. "Including the flower club's meeting schedule."

"My heart bleeds." She rolled her eyes. "Speaking of whom, looks like they're leaving. I'll get you a couple of chairs."

"Thanks." My attention returned to the flower club's table, where the witches had begun to get to their feet. A commotion arose when someone knocked over a nearly full mug of tea, and poor Rowan had to run and clean up the mess while the oblivious witches trailed out of the café without acknowledging her.

"Honestly." I crossed the room and sidestepped the weedy shifter barista to grab a chair for Dad and then another for me. As I did so, the shifters at the nearby table flagged Rowan down to order more drinks.

"Were those witches really planning to cheat in the contest?" Dad asked when I returned to the table with our chairs. "Not that I'm encouraging you to tell tales, but your mother would appreciate a heads-up, right?"

"I should report them, but I don't know how much of that was just talk." I planted my chair on one side of the table and sat down. "Why would anyone in the coven have got their hands on thorn-killer toxin in the first place?"

"I don't know," he said. "There are always some people who try to skirt the rules. I had this guy try to sell me a pile of cement the other day that he claimed was enhanced with an instant-sticking spell so I wouldn't have to wait for it to dry."

"That sounds like a disaster waiting to happen. What if you stuck your hand in it?"

"See, that's why I turned him down." Dad worked in construction on a freelance basis while helping Jessica take care of the kids the rest of the time. Mum and the coven might criticise my dad's lack of ambition, but if you asked me, he had a more fun lifestyle than being Head Witch. With much less peril, unless you counted eternally sticky cement.

"Good call," I said. "It might not have even worked."

"Oh, it worked," he said. "He told me later that they couldn't even get the cement out of the container."

I snickered. "That's what cheating brings you. Often, it's easier to just do things the right way."

Rowan walked past and dropped off the shifters' drinks at the nearby table before returning to ours. "Ah, crap. Sorry, I forgot your drinks."

"Don't apologise," I said to her. "We were delivering essential gossip."

She grinned and departed for the counter while Dad and I returned to our discussion.

"If anyone *did* cheat in the contest, Mum would shut them down," I said. "I'd have liked to think most people would be a bit more considerate, considering the event almost didn't go ahead at all."

We'd gone over the subject at length during our coven meetings. Some council members hadn't wanted the event to be open to the public outside of Wildwood Heath, while others wanted extra security. A couple had even suggested that I set up protective wards using my sceptre since it would be stronger than a ward cast with a wand, but Mum had shut that idea down so fast that I'd been torn between feeling relieved and insulted.

I thought I'd been making decent progress at using the sceptre to cast spells, thanks to lessons from my impatient grandmother's ghost, but the trouble with my magic being amplified a hundredfold was that any mistakes were too. If I tried to put up a protective spell around the town, there was a chance I'd encase us in a bubble by accident, and nobody would be able to get in at all. Better to leave it to the police instead. I figured that if someone wanted to kill me that badly, they'd find a way into town regardless of any defences we put up, and I was better off conserving my energy for the next inevitable confrontation.

As the thought crossed my mind, a choking noise made me spin around in my seat. One of the shifters—the guy who'd been boasting about his promotion to his bored friend—had begun to cough uncontrollably, and his cup fell from his hands as he slid from his seat.

"What's happening to him?" Dad rose to his feet, as did several other patrons, but the shifter's writhing and choking ceased almost as suddenly as it had started.

Rowan ducked out from behind the counter, pale-faced, while her colleague stood stock-still next to the fallen shifter. His companion stared, stunned, across the table, while someone screamed, breaking the silence. "He's dead!"

The door nudged open, and a flash of fluffy red tail cued Tansy's arrival as she came scurrying over to Dad and me.

"I can't leave you alone for five minutes, can I?" she said. "What happened this time?"

I shook my head, unwilling to draw attention. Not that the sceptre in my hand could have stopped someone from choking to death, but Tansy hopped off the table when I didn't answer and ran over to the shifter's body, sniffing at him.

The shifter's companion startled, shooing Tansy away with his hands. "Hey—get away from him."

"Excuse me?" Tansy puffed up her tail in indignation at being treated like a pest. "I'm trying to help. It looks like your friend was poisoned."

Since only Rowan and I could understand my familiar,

her words would sound like squeaking to everyone else. I didn't entirely blame the other shifter for looking wary, but more and more eyes began to turn in my direction. Whispers arose, cut through by the sound of the door opening. I rotated in that direction and saw a couple of customers in the process of leaving the café.

"Don't," I told them. "The police will want everyone to stay put."

My words brought some unwelcome mutters, accompanied with stares at my sceptre from anyone who hadn't already noticed. The stares only intensified when Tansy returned to our table, accompanied by a horrified-looking Rowan.

"I made the coffee myself," she whispered. "I don't understand."

"Neither do I." If she'd made the drink, how could the shifter have been poisoned?

The door opened again, this time from the outside, and the police entered the café. Specifically, my brother, Ramsey.

3

───────

When my brother walked in, the customers who'd been in the process of leaving the café hurriedly returned to their table. I'd thought he was busy on the other side of town, setting up the carnival, so I hadn't a clue how he'd arrived here so fast, but that was the least of my concerns. His gaze flickered with annoyance when he spotted Dad and me right next to the shifter's table, but I looked defiantly back. It didn't escape my attention that he avoided looking directly at Dad, whose shoulders slumped as he watched Ramsey walk past without acknowledging him.

My brother stopped beside the fallen shifter and asked the room at large, "What happened here?"

Several people started talking at once.

"He just fell out of his seat."

"He choked."

"She knows something." The shifter's companion pointed directly at me. "She was talking to that squirrel of hers."

Thanks a bunch.

Resigned, I faced my brother. "Tansy thinks he was poisoned, but his drink spilled when he fell out of his seat."

Ramsey eyed the cup the shifter had dropped. "I can still check for poison."

"What, you want us to get it into a bottle?" Rowan asked sceptically. "How're we supposed to do that?"

Ignoring her question, he asked, "Which of you made and served the drink?"

"I—I did," said Rowan, and my heart sank.

What if someone wanted her to take the blame?

Dad's wide eyes met mine as if he'd caught on to my line of thought, but Ramsey didn't even blink at Rowan's reply. "Tell me exactly what you did. You gave him the drink, and then...?"

"I was... well, talking to Robin." A flush lit her face.

"Is that so?" He gave me an accusing look, which struck me as a little unfair. It was hardly my fault that I seemingly couldn't even go out for a coffee without someone dropping dead.

"Yes," I said to Ramsey. "Did you want to interview us individually?"

A muscle twitched in his jaw as the other customers raised their voices in protest, but at least it took his attention off Rowan. And Dad, whose slumped posture was the only indication of his hurt feelings at Ramsey's refusal to acknowledge him. Dad might put on a brave face most of the time, but I knew it stung that his eldest child continued to reject him. How could it not? I'd made no secret of believing Mum was more to blame for the disintegration of their marriage, and yet we'd remained on speaking terms, but this wasn't the time to force Ramsey to get the hell over himself. Especially if the person who'd poisoned the shifter's coffee was here in this very room.

Who, though? This one had me stumped, especially as the only people who'd drawn my suspicion were the flower club witches, and they'd already left when the shifter had been served his drink. My attention went to his companion instead. *Did he have anything to do with this?* He was the obvious person to blame given his proximity to the victim, but he'd have had to employ some major sleight of hand to have poisoned someone who sat directly in front of him without being noticed. Then again, had the other shifter been paying attention at all when he'd been occupied with singing his own praises? I couldn't judge them both based on a single conversation, but if the police didn't have a single suspect, the blame might fall by default upon the person who'd served them their drinks.

When I looked at Rowan, the colour had drained from her face. I followed her line of sight to the back of the room, where her boss, Mal, had come out to see what was going on. The burly shifter's blond hair was buzzed short, and his broad shoulders suggested he worked with heavy machinery rather than running a coffee shop. Despite his fierce appearance, he treated Rowan and his other employees like family.

While Ramsey spoke to the boss, the baristas started cleaning up. Everyone gave the spilled drink a wide berth, and I found myself wishing I knew a spell to help detect poison. That would be more practical than trying to scoop it off the floor.

After a few minutes, two more officers showed up to move the shifter's body, at which point Ramsey returned to our table. "Robin, I'd like to hear your account of the events first."

At least he hadn't picked on Rowan, but murmurs and

whispers followed as he led me to a table at the back of the café.

"You want my account of events?" I sat down opposite him. "Like Rowan told you, my dad and I came to have coffee and were talking. Mostly about the carnival and the contest. Then that guy... he just dropped dead."

"I rather hoped you might have been more observant."

"I don't usually walk in here expecting to witness a murder, Ramsey."

"You were next to their table. Surely you heard something?"

I hesitated. "Look, I don't want an innocent person to be arrested because of something I heard out of context. Does eavesdropping even count as evidence?"

"That," he said, "depends on what exactly you heard."

"The shifter who died was bragging about his promotion," I recalled. "It sounded as if his acquaintance was passed over for the same job, which he seemed annoyed at. But I don't know that it's enough for him to commit murder."

"Tansy, did you see anything?" he asked my familiar, who'd climbed onto the table.

"No," she replied, her tail drooping. "I was outside, chasing pigeons."

Ramsey's eyes narrowed. "I see."

"This place was packed, Ramsey," I said. "Before the flower club left—which reminds me, they might be planning to cheat in the contest."

"What do you expect me to do about that?"

"Nothing," I said. "I thought you wanted to hear my account, though, and most of what I overheard came from them before they left the café."

"Did they have access to the victim's drink?"

"No." I hesitated. "Are you planning to ask for an account from everyone in here, including Rowan... and Dad?"

"Yes, or one of my fellow officers will." His tone was indifferent. "I'll wait and see what the other witnesses say before we decide whether to invite anyone to the office for further questioning."

While I understood that he was here in a professional capacity, part of me couldn't suppress a rush of irritation. "I realise the timing is atrocious, but you must see how messed up it is that the first one-on-one conversation you and Dad have had in years is going to involve questioning him about a murder."

"It's my job, Robin," he said predictably. "I can't let any biases get in the way."

"Okay, but you two should *actually* talk afterwards—"

"That's enough." He rose to his feet. "Send Rowan to talk to me next, won't you?"

Giving up, I walked back to tell my cousin the unwelcome news. *Honestly.* Ramsey in work mode was even worse than the everyday one. At least with the latter, I occasionally saw glimmers of the person whom I'd grown up chasing around the woodlands and climbing trees with—though not that often, since he'd been positively middle-aged since he could walk, and Mum had only encouraged him. It was ridiculous.

"Your brother is questioning everyone?" asked Dad.

"Looks that way," I replied. "Listen... don't take anything he says personally. When he's in professional-officer mode, he tends to get a bit intense."

"I figured," he said wryly. "Don't worry about me, Robin. I won't make this any more difficult for Ramsey than it already is."

"Oh, he's in his element here." To Rowan, I added, "Sorry. You're next."

My nerves raced as my cousin crossed the room, especially when I caught sight of her boss watching her from near the counter. One of the officers had scooped the remains of the poisoned drink into a container, while the shifter's companion remained in the same spot, not meeting anyone's eyes. *He has to be high on the suspect list, right?*

Rowan's questioning was over surprisingly fast, and she stopped near the shifter's companion to point him towards Ramsey's table next. When she returned to my side, she wore a subdued expression. "I should have known this was too good to be true."

"What do you mean?" I asked. "You aren't going to be blamed for this. Anyone can see it wasn't your fault. Ramsey didn't suggest otherwise, did he?"

"No, but he made it clear I should have been more observant."

"He said the same to me," I said. "It's a special line he reserves for family members."

Her head drooped. "Maybe, but if we end up losing business over this, the other staff won't be happy."

"Would your boss really blame you?"

"I'd like to think not," she mumbled. "But if this turns out to be linked to the coven?"

"Meaning your mother?" I spoke in an undertone. "It can't be, surely."

"My mum's familiar has been hanging around the café again," she admitted. "I've seen Myrtle sitting on the windowsill three times in the past week."

"What's she playing at?" I thought Aunt Shannon had got the message to leave her youngest daughter alone after the pair of us had confronted her in person—a major milestone for Rowan, who'd made it clear that she wouldn't be coming back to the coven. Did my aunt want to ensure that her youngest daughter was behaving herself, or did she have other motives?

As for the timing? Most of the police force was currently on the other side of town, which Aunt Shannon certainly knew, but even if she'd had a hand in this, she couldn't possibly have been certain that her daughter would be the one to make the poisoned drink.

"Haven't a clue," said Rowan. "Maybe she sent Myrtle to remind me of her existence, as if I can forget it."

I watched the victim's companion cross the café towards the back corner. "If anyone did it, it's him, though I don't know how he would have poisoned the drink in plain sight."

"Nor me, but even Ralph wasn't watching."

"I was asleep," said a muffled voice as her tarantula familiar poked a hairy leg out of her sleeve.

"Hey, Ralph." I peered at the tarantula. "I didn't know you were here."

"I have to hide him when I'm working," Rowan said. "He doesn't like staying in my room alone, but Richie is terrified of spiders. So are some of our customers."

"I'm more scared of them than they are of me." Ralph's muffled voice came from her sleeve. "I don't want to go to jail."

"Neither of you is going to jail," I whispered "They'll find the real culprit. Besides, Ramsey won't lock up his own cousin."

I think. One never really knew with Ramsey, and when Dad was called in for questioning next, he stiffened.

"Good luck." I gave him a quick hug before he crossed the room. To Rowan, I whispered, "I feel bad for him. What a way to get back in touch with your stubborn offspring."

"That's Ramsey's fault, not your dad's," said Rowan.

"And Mum's. They're both as set in their ways as a concrete broomstick." Mum's initial response to their divorce had been to ban Dad from seeing either of us, and while Dad had done his best to get around that by employing Tansy to carry messages to us and leave presents outside our rooms, Ramsey had refused to acknowledge him and had maintained his stubbornness to this day.

I tried to watch Dad and Ramsey's faces, but I couldn't see Ramsey's expression from this far off. It seemed like no time at all before Dad got to his feet again and crossed the café to join us.

"How'd it go?" I asked.

"About as well as possible, considering," he said. "I told him everything I saw, and that was that."

I hadn't really expected otherwise despite the tiny part of me that held out hope for forgiveness on Ramsey's part.

"If you've been questioned, you can leave," said one of the other officers.

"I can't," Rowan answered. "I *live* here."

I cleared my throat. "I ought to stay. Just in case I'm needed."

"I understand," said Dad. "I have to work this afternoon, but text me later, okay?"

"Sure." I hugged him goodbye, and before he left, he briefly glanced over at Ramsey. My brother had definitely seen our interaction, but he gave us no further acknowledgement. That figured.

After Dad had left, I waited with Rowan for the police to get through questioning the rest of the suspects. With three officers present, it took less time than I expected, and soon, we were the only people left in the room.

Ramsey returned to the front of the café and halted in front of me. "Robin, *why* are you still here?"

"It's Saturday, Ramsey. I don't have anywhere else to be."

"The café is going to close for the rest of the day," he said. "I expect the owner will ask you to leave even if you refuse to listen to me."

I knew when I was beaten, so I turned to Rowan. "Sorry."

"I'll be fine." She glanced nervously over at her boss. "Hell of a way to get the day off, but I might as well make the most of it."

"Yeah. I'll drop by later."

"After closing time," she agreed. "We can still have a gaming night."

"Of course." Her boss wouldn't punish her for something that quite clearly wasn't her fault, would he? Neither of us had been the killer's intended target, so it couldn't be tied back to our family... unless her mother *had* been involved.

Let's face it—I couldn't entirely rule out the possibility, which meant I had to do everything I could to help the police, however little Ramsey wanted me to stick around.

After leaving, I waited outside the café until Ramsey emerged with his fellow officers. Upon spotting me, he sighed. "Robin, I told you to go back home. This isn't a matter for the Head Witch to involve herself in."

"I was here, which means I'm involved by default," I countered. "We can't entirely dismiss the possibility that I was the intended target, can we?"

"Do you think you were?" He arched a brow. "If you thought so, you should have brought it up earlier."

"I don't, but there *is* a chance that Rowan's mother is up to her old tricks."

Tansy scampered up my arm to perch on my shoulder. "Rowan said that magpie's been hanging around. Should I go and look for her?"

"Not yet." I looked straight at my brother's disapproving face. "You have to admit it's possible that Aunt Shannon is scheming new ways to ruin her daughter's life."

"You think she wants to get revenge by murdering a stranger?" he asked in sceptical tones.

"I admit the chances are slim, but it's better to be safe than sorry, right?"

"Robin, that's usually the opposite of your approach."

"Harsh," I said. "Look, I'm not going to get under your feet. You never know; I might even be able to help you find out who did it. Wouldn't be the first time."

He hesitated for a long moment. "If you aren't going to let this drop, you can come with me when I talk to the victim's companion again tomorrow. On the condition that starting Monday, you return to your duties as Head Witch."

"Excellent," I said. "I'll be right there."

Ramsey looked me over, a frown on his face. "Don't make me regret this."

4

———

The following morning, Tansy woke me up by tickling my nose with her fluffy tail. I sneezed, rolling onto my side. "Tansy, it's Sunday morning."

"Didn't you say you'd help your brother question that shifter dude?"

I groaned. "Right, right."

I'd forgotten to set an alarm since I'd stayed out late at Rowan's place and hadn't slept well after I'd come back. Rowan and I had tried to unwind by playing video games, though we'd both been too unsettled by the events of the previous day to entirely enjoy ourselves. I'd also messaged Harvey, telling him about the murder in case word reached him via the town's rumour mill, though he hadn't replied yet. Admittedly, I'd turned off my phone for most of the previous evening to avoid certain family members trying to contact me while I was at Rowan's.

I picked out an inoffensive outfit—with the exception of my socks, which depicted Pikachu on a surfboard—and went downstairs to find my brother. To my relief, he hadn't left without me and, instead, sat at the kitchen table, where

Kimberly, the family chef, had set out a veritable feast of a fried breakfast. Ramsey was sipping black coffee and not eating anything—a waste if you asked me—so I deliberately loaded up my plate.

Kimberly beamed at me, but Ramsey's jaw twitched when I sat opposite him. "We'll have to leave in less than an hour if you want to come with me."

"You don't think I can eat that fast?" I shot him a grin. "Challenge accepted."

"I know you can, but I thought you were trying to behave with a little more decorum than when you were a teenager." He grimaced when I shoved a huge piece of bacon into my mouth.

I made a point of chewing and swallowing before I said, "Not at home. Besides, I expect you'll keep me run off my feet all day."

I was a little surprised he'd agreed to let me help at all, though I suspected that he'd redact that decision if I so much as mentioned the possibility of him interacting with Dad again, even as a potential suspect in the shifter's death.

"Hardly," he said. "We have one suspect on the list who merits a second questioning: Dale Longfoot, the man who was closest to the victim when he died. The rest of the day, I'll spend in my office, and I think you'd prefer not to stay and help out."

"Meaning you don't want me messing up all your paperwork?" I quipped. "No, thanks. I spend entirely too much time in an office as it is."

I did too. My new job was entirely too sedentary for my liking, and if I kept eating like this, I'd need to take up some active hobby if I wanted to continue to fit into my tailored Head Witch clothes. I could only imagine what kind of disaster I might unleash if I tried to apply my sceptre's magic to resizing my clothes.

After I'd cleared my plate, Ramsey and I left the house. While Tansy kept us entertained by chasing off any bird that dared to cross her path, Ramsey and I retained a neutral silence, since I didn't quite trust myself not to mention Dad if I opened my mouth. When we reached the centre of town, the first thing I saw was the Closed sign in the window of Were's My Coffee?, and a pang hit me. I'd seen the café closed up for the night countless times before, of course, but this was different.

Then another thought hit me. "If the café stays closed, where will the tourists visiting the carnival go to get their coffee?"

"There are stalls selling coffee at the carnival, Robin," he said. "They'll be fine."

"But it's not the same." I sighed. "Were's My Coffee? is an experience that can't be replicated."

"I'm sure they'll reopen tomorrow." He walked on. "They need the business. I'd also prefer for no more negative attention to fall on our family."

"Might be hoping for too much there," I said. "Wait, do you really think Rowan is going to take the blame for this? I thought she wasn't a suspect."

"She isn't, but as no witnesses came forward to say how the poison might have got into the victim's drink, we can't ignore the fact that she's the one who made it. I know," he added. "I know she doesn't have any possible reason to murder one of her customers, but I wouldn't be doing my job if I cut her from the list of suspects solely for being a family member."

I scowled. "Better hope we get something good from this guy we're visiting, then. Do you know where he lives?"

"Yes," he said. "He started working at the same company as Linus—the victim—several months before Linus joined up."

"You've looked into his background? Or is that what he told you yesterday?"

"Both," he said. "I looked into his background after I got back to the office, as well as checking up on the carnival security."

"You know it's not compulsory for you to do everything yourself?" I reminded him. "Especially at the weekend."

"Murderers don't take weekends off. Evidently."

"Ha." He hadn't intended to be funny, but that was typical of my brother. He worked until he keeled over if someone didn't intervene. "You need an assistant if you ask me. I wonder if Mum knows of anyone else she can recommend. Like Chloe." My assistant had saved my sanity on more than one occasion since I'd become Head Witch.

"I do *not* need an assistant, Robin," he said. "I'm perfectly capable of handling everything myself."

I could tell I was going to end up losing that argument, so I dropped the subject for now.

Ramsey led the way to a row of terraced houses and knocked on the right door, while I stood at his side and tried not to look too intimidating. Evidently, I didn't do a great job, because the shifter who answered the door went deathly pale at the sight of me.

"Head Witch," he croaked. "Ah... you're helping the police?"

"Sort of." My brother shot me a warning look, so I fell silent and let him speak.

"Dale Longfoot," Ramsey said. "May I come in?"

"Sure." He shuffled back into the hallway and showed us into a living room that looked neater than your average bachelor pad, as if he'd tidied up in anticipation of a visit from the police.

He sat in an armchair, keeping one eye on my sceptre as if it were a bomb about to go off. Wariness around the Head Witch didn't necessarily point to guilt on his part, but it was a bit ridiculous. The shifter was a good six feet tall and looked like he actually used the weightlifting machines visible through an open door to an adjoining room, and really, if he'd wanted to commit murder, he could probably have snapped the other guy's neck with his forearm *without* shifting into a werewolf.

Not that Ramsey seemed to care what I thought. He launched straight into the usual list of questions concerning Dale's companion's unfortunate fate.

"You and Linus Tooley were co-workers," Ramsey said. "Linus received a recent promotion to a role that you were hoping to be considered for, is that correct?"

"Yeah." His shoulders slumped. "I know it looks bad, but what would committing murder achieve? It's hardly going to make my boss pay me any more attention."

"Where do you work?"

"In an insurance office. Not glamorous, I know, but the pay's good."

I suppressed a yawn by clenching my jaw and wishing I'd brought a coffee—a thought that reminded me of the sad sight of Were's My Coffee?'s closed door and dampened my mood even further. It was abundantly clear that I was of no help in this situation and that I might as well have stayed in bed.

When my brother had finally exhausted all the possible questions on Dale and Linus's work life, I seized the chance to ask one of my own. "Dale, did you see anyone near your table at the café when Linus died?"

He tensed. His manner had relaxed a little when I'd let Ramsey take over the questioning, but the wariness returned when I spoke and reminded him of my presence.

"No," he replied. "I... I wasn't really paying attention. He kept talking, and to be honest, I'd zoned out."

Ramsey's jaw twitched in irritation, but I was pretty sure he'd been heading down that road himself with his questioning, and I'd just brought him to the point sooner. Not that we'd actually learned anything of note.

My brother reached the end of the interview in short order, and Dale watched us leave with an expression of barely concealed relief. As we walked out of the house and the door closed behind us, Ramsey frowned to himself as if lost in thought.

"What do you think?" I asked him.

"Huh?"

"About him?" I jerked my head towards the shifter's house. "Think he's a murderer?"

"Oh." He paused. "No... well, it's not up to me to make judgements until I've gathered more evidence, but so far, he hasn't said anything that would merit further investigation. I intend to talk to his employer tomorrow, while some of our officers are looking into the precise poison that was used on the victim. So far, they've concluded that it's not a commonly identifiable poison."

"Which means... what?"

"The poison appears to have been brewed rather than given in the form of raw ingredients," he elaborated. "A few crushed leaves of a deadly plant would have sufficed, but whoever did this went a step further."

"Weird," I commented. "That makes it seem less likely that guy did it. I don't see him brewing a poison from scratch, do you?"

"I haven't a clue." He stifled a yawn behind his hand.

"You need a nap if you ask me," I told him. "You weren't even supposed to be at work today."

"I could say the same of you."

"Shouldn't that be 'you're welcome'?" I raised a brow at him. "I know, I'm no investigator. I hoped we'd get more clues from him, and I didn't expect him to be that scared of my sceptre either."

"You shouldn't have expected him to overlook your presence," he said. "Bringing the Head Witch with me sends a clear message, and so does your interest in the investigation."

"The message is that I want my cousin to catch a break for once." *And that I want you to stop being a stubborn nuisance when it comes to our dad,* I added silently. "You ought to know that people will make their own assumptions regardless. If I kept my distance, some people would assume I didn't care about witnessing a murder."

He shook his head. "That's not the same. Besides, the timing of this incident isn't ideal, with most of my team currently occupied with setting up security around the carnival."

"You think someone took advantage?" I'd wondered about the timing myself.

"Unlikely, but I have to consider all the variables, including the possibility that others are waiting for us to let down our guard."

"Even you can't be in two places at once," I added. "Unless you multitask by inviting the potential suspects to be questioned while you're *at* the carnival."

"Certainly not."

"That wasn't serious, Ramsey. Though Dad's cottage is right by the field—joking, joking," I said hastily as he glared at me. "Look, Dad is happy to keep his distance if that's what you want, but what happens if you do have to pay him a home visit?"

"I'll do whatever I have to in order to get answers," he said. "Besides, my team knows I'm impartial."

"Okay, fine, have it your way." I knew it would annoy him, but I added, "I'll let him know you might drop by. It's only fair that he's prepared."

"You're not going to tell him everything I've told you, are you?" His eyes narrowed. "It's against the rules to discuss ongoing investigations with civilians."

"He's family, Ramsey." I didn't expect that comment to be met with anything but another disapproving glare, but I couldn't hold my tongue a moment longer. "And he's a witness."

"Go home, Robin." He veered away from me, heading down the main street for the police station without looking back.

That went well. I should have known better than to push his buttons, but I'd dragged myself out of bed to help him out, and I couldn't even buy a latte from Were's My Coffee? on the way back.

As I retraced my steps towards home, my phone began to buzz in my pocket. When I checked, I found an unknown number was calling me. *Please tell me it isn't the bloody press again.*

"Yes?" I answered tersely.

"Robin," said Harvey's voice. "Sorry, I should have given you this number before. I'm calling from my landline."

"Oh, sorry," I said. "Wait, what happened to your phone?"

"There was an, uh, incident yesterday when I was flying."

It took a moment for my tired brain to process that. "Did you forget to take your phone out of your pocket before you got on your broomstick?"

"Yes, and I had to fish it out of a pond." He sounded vaguely embarrassed. "Yours is fine, isn't it? I tried calling you yesterday, but it went to voicemail."

"Yeah... sorry, I turned it off to avoid my family pestering me while I was at Rowan's," I said. "Did you get my message?"

"That's what I was calling about," he said. "You said someone was poisoned at the café? Not Were's My Coffee...?"

"Unfortunately, yes." I filled him in on the disaster that had been my weekend so far, finishing with my attempt to help Ramsey question the sole suspect. Knowing my brother would doubtless be even less thrilled at me for telling my boyfriend the details of the ongoing investigation didn't lessen my desire to vent my frustration to someone impartial.

Despite what some people might have thought, Harvey had nothing to gain from dating the Head Witch but a great deal of potential hassle. As Dad's situation proved, being entangled with my family didn't even end when a relationship did, though I was of the firm belief that Harvey and I were going to stick together for the long haul regardless of the obstacles the universe saw fit to throw at us.

"Bad timing," he commented. "I saw them setting up the carnival over in the field. Looked impressive."

"None of my work, believe me," I said. "Mum wouldn't let me help. She nearly got in a fight with her sister when *she* offered to help, though accepting a gift from my aunt is like hosting a children's birthday party at Jurassic Park."

"Ha." I heard the smile in his voice. "So... you're okay, then?"

"*I* am," I said. "It's Rowan I'm concerned for. She's worried her boss might decide that offering employment and accommodation to one of the Wildwood family is more trouble than it's worth."

"How can he possibly blame her?" he asked. "Surely it's just bad luck that she made the drink that killed the shifter. There's no way she can have been involved."

"Her mother might have," I said in a low voice. "There's a slim chance, mind, but I can't entirely dismiss the possibility. She's still sending her familiar to spy on Rowan even after we warned her not to."

"You'd think she'd have learned her lesson."

"She doesn't like to lose. Runs in the family."

I was an exception, having inherited the bare minimum of my family's competitive nature. That was probably for the best, because otherwise, I'd have no self-esteem left. Rowan was the same, but she'd had a far rougher time of it than I had, and I refused to watch her lose the life she'd started to build on her own terms without her mother's involvement.

"What're you doing today, anyway?" Harvey asked. "I wish I could come and see you, but I have another practise session this afternoon. We rearranged the schedule due to the carnival."

"Oops," I said. "Sorry. You can blame that one on my family."

"We have to do the same every year. It's fine," he said. "But I can tell you need time to decompress. I don't know if you want to watch us practise, but it's not the same as spending time together as just the two of us."

"Well... my dad's at home." With Jessica and the kids, but that didn't matter. "I'll see you... sometime next week?

It'd be nice to go to the carnival, but knowing my luck, my mother will have me running errands."

Which was better than helping at the flower contest but not by much.

"I hope we can meet up there," he said. "Also, I should have a new phone within a couple days if the repair shop can't perform a miracle and fix the old one."

"I've been practising drying spells, but you might need something more precise." If I tried to use my sceptre to remove pond water from his phone, I risked causing a small explosion. Magic and technology didn't always mix that well.

"Don't worry about it," he said. "Go and enjoy the rest of your day."

"I'll try to." I smiled. "Thanks, Harvey. See you soon."

"Bye." He ended the call while I walked straight past my family's home to the path leading into the forest and to my dad's cottage. There was no day that couldn't be improved by a game of football with a pair of rambunctious shifter kids, and as a bonus, I'd have a view of Harvey's practise session from the garden.

If it annoyed Ramsey that I fully intended on telling Dad everything it wasn't my problem. Even the Head Witch was allowed to have fun occasionally.

5

"If you keep waving that sceptre so close to those papers, you're going to set them on fire," Grandma told me.

I swung the sceptre away, narrowly missing hitting my assistant in the face. "We should have gone outside, Grandma, I told you. Sorry, Chloe."

Chloe, whose attention hadn't slipped from her laptop screen even when she'd had to duck to avoid my sceptre, answered without looking up. "Don't worry about it."

How my assistant could focus on work while I was learning magic from my grandmother's ghost right in front of her, I had no idea whatsoever, but her impressive efficiency came in handy. Especially since I was somewhat lacking in that department myself.

"If you had better control, it wouldn't be a problem" was Grandma's unhelpful reply.

The lesson was actually going pretty well, at least compared to my usual standards, since I'd managed to use the right spell. Yes, my aim needed improvement, but waving a massive stick inside a cramped office without knocking into things was an exercise in futility. It didn't help that Grandma had insisted I needed to hold the sceptre in one hand and not both, further unbalancing me.

"Nobody told me I'd have to take up weightlifting to become Head Witch." I rubbed my sore shoulder with my free hand. At this rate, my right arm, but not my left, would be as bulky as the average shifter's. "Right, right. I'll try again."

The sceptre was typically used as a show of prestige, and it'd taken a fair bit of persuasion to convince my grandmother to start training me to use magic with it. She wasn't exactly the most patient teacher, and when she reached out to correct my grip, I shuddered so hard at her clammy ghost's touch that I narrowly avoided dropping the sceptre on the floor.

"Grandma, seriously." I backed out of her reach. "That's not helping."

"You need to learn to stop waving that sceptre around like a drunken scarecrow."

"Thanks a bunch." I might have added that I'd looked considerably more coordinated at the start of our session, before my arm had turned to jelly. "Call it a work in progress. I got the first spell right, didn't I?"

"That's not going to matter in a real-life scenario, is it?" she said. "The enemy won't wait for you to have a lucky streak."

She might have had a point, but I didn't think it was that controversial to want to take note of the progress I'd made rather than dwelling on my legion of mistakes. "If I was duelling, I'd go straight for a freeze-frame spell first."

"You can't rely on just one spell, Robin."

"It works, and I don't see why I should mess with a good thing." Grandma always had an argument for me, but

I had to admit verbally sparring with her made my job infinitely more interesting than if I'd been trapped behind a desk all day. Even if it was slightly more hazardous than the typical office job... though perhaps more for my co-workers than me. Chloe and I had had to put out several literal fires in the past few weeks, and I'd found myself incredibly glad that my assistant had taken to storing important paperwork online instead of keeping everything in hard copy.

Grandma tutted. "Have it your way. Go back to your desk, and I expect you to have that spell perfectly mastered by tomorrow."

"When exactly am I supposed to practise?" I asked. "I'll be at the carnival from the instant I finish work until sundown."

"Work it out. We all have the same twenty-four hours a day." She drifted out of sight, vanishing among the cabinets at the back of the office.

"Some of us need sleep," I said to the spot where she'd been floating. "Guess there have to be a few perks to being dead."

A pen threw itself at me. I caught it in my free hand, my instincts in fine form after weeks of dealing with Grandma's antics after she'd discovered she could lift objects into the air like a poltergeist. Every other day, I came into work to find she'd entirely rearranged the furniture in a fit of overnight boredom. She claimed the office was more hers than mine since she'd been here first, and I had yet to win that argument. Still, it was a relatively small price to pay for being able to keep the former Head Witch on as an unofficial consultant.

I returned to my desk and checked the time. "Great. Another council meeting in half an hour."

"Need me to prepare anything?" Chloe asked. "I already have a list of notes."

"When on earth did you have time to write up those?"

I could have sworn she had an extra five hours or so tucked away each day that the rest of us didn't have access to. That, or she didn't sleep, but unlike Grandma, she was very much alive. She and my brother would get on well if they ever stopped working long enough to take notice of one another.

"Last night," she answered. "It's mostly going to be a repeat of the same issues as last week though, isn't it? Safety concerns around the carnival, the flower contest..."

I groaned. "Aunt Shannon is going to monopolise that discussion again; I just know it. Did she and Mum ever come to an agreement over the stage, do you know?"

"I believe they borrowed a stage from the town hall."

"So Aunt Shannon won?" She'd be even more insufferable than usual if she had. "Unless everyone thinks it was Mum's idea. Did she manage to spread word around the rest of the council in time?"

Her brow wrinkled. "I don't know, but I'm sure you'll find out at the meeting."

"I'm waiting with bated breath." Honestly, there were far more useful things I might have been doing with my time. I hadn't even been able to check in with Ramsey yet, since he'd gone straight to the office before I'd properly woken up that morning, so I didn't know how the investigation was progressing. I didn't think he'd paid any more home visits, at least. I debated messaging Dad to ask, but I didn't need to further sink my name in the eyes of the coven by having my phone go off in the middle of a meeting.

"The contest is tomorrow, so it's not going to be the main

topic for long," said Chloe. "They'll move on to something else by the end of the week."

"Unless Aunt Shannon wins."

Her head lifted. "You don't think she will, do you?"

"I don't." Mum would make sure of that. "I *do* think she's trying to get one up on Mum by weaselling her way into the carnival planning. I'd also like to know why she still has her familiar spying on Rowan."

My familiar had offered to watch Myrtle to make sure she didn't go anywhere near the café or Rowan, but if Aunt Shannon had somehow been involved in Saturday's incident, I was still at a loss to explain why or how. Let alone what she had to gain from spying on her daughter.

"Strange," Chloe commented. "It might be nothing, though. She's part of the coven, too, after all, and on the council as well."

"I doubt she was trying to get involved in the carnival out of a desire to serve her coven and to give back to the community."

When the meeting time rolled around, I left my office and walked the short distance across the lobby to the meeting room. Mum already sat in her place, so I took a seat beside her while the other council members of the coven gathered around the table. I was the youngest aside from my cousin Vanessa, who looked almost identical to her mother and wore a mirror of her customary scowl when I called the meeting to a start.

"The carnival will open to visitors from outside Wildwood Heath later this afternoon," I told the council members. "Lady Wildwood tells me that everything is set up as planned."

It was still weird as hell to call my mother by her title in front of the council, as if I was talking about a stranger and not the person who'd told Tansy off for sitting in the butter dish at breakfast that morning.

"Correct," said Mum. "The flower tent is all set up, and the only thing left to arrange is the evening's firework display."

"Who is in charge of the fireworks?" Aunt Shannon wanted to know.

"I have a team of volunteers prepared," she said. "They'll start after the winner's speech. I trust that will be adequate?"

Everyone nodded except for my aunt. "And do you have an alternative plan?" she asked. "It seems unwise to plan the entire carnival around the assumption that the same person will win the contest as every other year."

A murmur arose among the other witches. She hadn't meant to imply that she expected to win the contest herself, had she? *If she did, then she's deluding herself.*

"Isn't that tradition?" I addressed the council, ignoring my aunt's glare at my interruption. Nothing mattered to the coven more than traditions, and even those who thought I wasn't the best pick for Head Witch wouldn't be able to argue with that.

"Yes, it is," said another witch. "On the subject of the refreshments…"

To my relief, the meeting ended without any more major conflicts, and Aunt Shannon and Vanessa were the first to depart. Nothing new there, but Mum stayed behind until everyone else had left the room.

"Robin," said Mum. "I want you to come with me to the field this afternoon."

Huh? "Why? I thought you wanted me to go through some of the backlog of correspondence."

"I'd appreciate your assistance with some last-minute preparations for the carnival."

"Well, since you asked so nicely." I frowned. "What's the issue?"

Your sister? I wanted to ask, but Aunt Shannon or her familiar might be listening in from outside the room. Her comments on the potential change in the contest's winner must have hit a nerve, but it was equally possible that Mum just wanted me to help with a last-minute security check before the first visitors from outside Wildwood Heath showed up. The carnival was technically her job more than it was mine, but I was glad of the chance to get outside the office.

"Simply caution." She swept out of the meeting room, and I hurried after her. "We'll head there now."

"It's my lunch break now, isn't it?" I reminded her. "I was going to drop by the café..."

"You can grab lunch from the carnival instead," she said. "It won't kill you."

I'd been more interested in checking up on Rowan, but I knew better than to argue with Mum when she was in one of these moods. I went to fetch Tansy and found her stalking a pigeon in the coven's back garden. The bird took flight in alarm when I walked outside, so Tansy came bounding over to me.

"No trouble from the magpie?" I asked her.

"No," she said. "She was digging up worms from the flowerbeds and ignoring me until she flew off a minute ago."

"I wonder where she went." I could guess. "Mum wants us to supervise the carnival. Meaning Aunt Shannon."

"What's she done now?"

"Nothing... yet," I clarified. "I'm not complaining about getting to spend a bit of time outside after all morning in that stuffy office."

"That can't have been fun." She scampered into the

building behind me, and we joined Mum in the lobby. Her own familiar was probably napping. Horace wasn't particularly involved in coven business, though to be honest, Tansy wasn't either. Unless driving meddling pigeons out of the garden counted as coven business.

"The visitors won't start arriving for another hour or two, right?" I asked Mum as we approached the woodland trail that led to the field.

"No, which is why we need to make sure the area is as secure as possible," she said without slowing her pace.

"I thought the police already put warding spells around the whole field."

Instead of answering, she continued down the path until we emerged from the forest into the carnival's field. Aunt Shannon was already there, standing in our line of sight... and beside her was a colossal yellow tent that hadn't been there the previous day. When she saw us approaching, she positioned herself in front of the tent's opening as if to prevent us from peering inside.

"What are you doing?" Mum demanded, marching over to her. "What is this?"

"I've taken your advice to heart," she said. "I decided to set up a tent of my own instead of treading on your feet."

"What exactly is in that tent?"

As Mum spoke, Tansy crept forward on careful feet, her tail sticking up and her attention on the smallest of gaps between the tent and the grassy floor.

"It's a surprise," said Aunt Shannon. "Don't look at me like that. It's perfectly within the regulations, which you'll know if you've read them recently."

Mum bristled. "I imagine I know the regulations better than you do, Shannon, and either you're a part of *my* event or you're a direct competitor. There are no other options."

"Then it's a good job I have permission from the mayor, isn't it?"

Tansy leapt back with a hiss when Myrtle landed in front of her, preventing her from going any closer to the tent.

"No peeking," said Aunt Shannon in a singsong voice.

Damn her. She's enjoying this.

Mum moved forward, reaching for her wand, but I caught her arm and hissed, "Mum, we're in public."

"As she knows full well." She shook me off and pulled out her wand, and my grip tightened on my sceptre. I could blast that tent sky-high without even thinking, as my aunt knew well, but she must have been counting on my reluctance to make a public scene. That was a dangerous gamble to take, given that my mother seemed to have cast her own reluctance aside.

"Really," said Aunt Shannon. "This is unnecessary. The contents of my tent have been verified by the mayor himself as being within the regulations."

If that was true, we didn't have any reason to worry. Yes, she'd overstepped by setting up her tent directly next to Mum's, but she wouldn't do anything to sabotage the rest of the carnival, surely.

"Mum, can we drop it?" I said in an undertone. "She's petty enough to argue this one to the ends of the earth, and there's such a thing as picking your battles wisely."

"This one is worth it," she said. "Besides, you don't have to get involved yourself, Robin."

"I'm involved by default in every single petty argument concerning our coven, whether it's actually relevant to me or not," I muttered. "What's the harm in her having her own section of the carnival? Isn't it better that she's out of our hair?"

Her lips thinned. "If anything goes wrong, it's on me."

"And me." I glanced over at my aunt, who wore a smirk on her face. "You know she wouldn't do anything out in the open. She's sneakier than that. Focus on the flower contest instead."

I knew my aunt could hear every word I said, but I didn't care. Part of me wanted to confront her about her familiar's habit of spying on Rowan while I was at it, but first, I needed to get my mother to loosen her grip on her wand before our visitors showed up to find two of the coven's most powerful witches ready to start a duel.

"If I find that your plans interfere with the contest or otherwise affect the rest of the carnival, then I'll have to take action." Mum gave her sister a thin-lipped glare before walking away towards the flower tent with me following behind.

"Speaking of interference in the contest," I added in a low voice, "did Ramsey mention the flower club met up at the café right before the murder?"

"They *what?*"

"He didn't tell you." I sighed inwardly. "Can I talk to you alone for a moment?"

Mum halted near the opening to the flower tent. "This had better be important."

"It is," I said. "When I was at the café on Saturday, I overheard a conversation between some elderly witches. They were discussing the contest, and one of them boasted about having got her hands on some kind of toxin... a thorn-killing toxin or something."

"Thorn-killer toxin?" She swivelled to face me. "Why didn't you tell me earlier?"

"Because someone dropped dead a few minutes after they left the café," I said. "I told Ramsey right away, and I assumed he'd tell you himself. Also—the witch said she got this toxin from someone in the coven."

"Well, *that* is abject nonsense," she said. "Nobody in the coven would stoop low enough to buy an illegal substance to ensure their victory in the contest, and we have stringent tests to detect cheating. Anyway, your brother has scarcely been at home in days."

"Thanks to the murder." Suspicion gripped me. "I don't know if there's any connection between the two, since the flower club members left *before* the guy dropped dead…"

"Put it out of your mind, Robin," she said. "Leave the murder investigation to your brother, and I'll handle the contest myself. You focus on your job as Head Witch."

"You're the one who just reprimanded me for not telling you what I overheard at the café," I pointed out. "Also, you haven't told me what you brought me here to do."

"I intended for you to check up on the security around the field, but that was before I found my sister bending the rules." She reached into her pocket for her phone. "I'll have to inform the contest's judges."

"Tell them someone might be planning to cheat in the contest too," I said to her. "Also, I wouldn't dismiss the possibility that the witch *did* get the toxin from someone in the coven."

Meaning Aunt Shannon. If anyone would be petty enough to apply a plant-killing toxin to her rivals' roses, it was my aunt. If she had proof, might it be inside the tent? I knew better than to think either Tansy or I would be able to simply walk in through the opening, but there had to be a way to get around her.

"I'm going to grab a coffee," I said to Mum. "I'll be right back."

I strode around the corner and slowed outside the

yellow monstrosity that comprised my aunt's latest scheme. Try as I might, I couldn't see a thing through the tent's fabric walls.

Tansy edged closer, sniffing at the tent's supporting posts. "I bet I can crawl through here."

"Not while she's in there." I approached the opening and stopped in my tracks when Myrtle the magpie flew into my face. Getting the message, I backed off and walked around the tent's right-hand side, Tansy scampering along behind me. "Might have to wait until she's gone."

"I'll look for a way in." Tansy sat on guard beside the tent while I bought a coffee and sandwich from a nearby stall, racking my brain for possible ways to enter my aunt's tent without tripping any alarm spells she might have set up. If I used my sceptre, it would be easy, but "subtle" wasn't exactly in the sceptre's handbook. Nor did I have a handbook at all, come to that. If I blew up the tent, my aunt would try to have me slapped with a fine for criminal damage.

"Robin."

I spun on my heel to see Ramsey approaching me. Oh boy.

6

———

"Ramsey." I faced my brother, whose smart suit looked somewhat out of place amid all the cheery tents. "Here for the carnival?"

"No," he said. "I was looking for our mother, actually. It's urgent."

"She was right there." I pointed around the corner of Aunt Shannon's tent. "Notice anything different?"

"I'll find her."

I'll take that as a no, then. I followed him around the tent, wondering how on earth he'd managed to overlook that bright-yellow monstrosity. It was awkward as hell trying to carry a coffee and sandwich and keep my grip on the sceptre at the same time, I might add. You'd think past Head Witches would have found a way to handle that, but maybe they just never left their headquarters. Grandma certainly hadn't.

Rounding a corner, I caught him up. "She was on the phone to the council the last time I saw her."

"Really?" He turned to me. "Why was she calling the council?"

"Because of that." I pointed to Aunt Shannon's tent. "Our aunt has been scheming. I thought Mum might have told you."

"I'm not here for our aunt," he said. "I'm here to ask if the judges at the flower contest are aware of any of their entrants might have got their hands on a bottle of thorn-killer toxin."

"Any *what?*" I blinked at him. "Didn't I tell you those witches were discussing in the café... wait, why?"

"Because," he said, "thorn-killer toxin is highly poisonous to humans when ingested."

Oh no. "It wasn't used to poison that shifter, was it?"

"You aren't to tell anyone else that, Robin, is that clear?"

My mouth parted. "I think that broomstick's already taken flight. Also, those flower club witches were discussing their plans out in the open."

"Tell me everything you heard them say," he said. "Every word."

"I didn't hear every word. I had to hide behind another table in case they recognised me." I briefly summed up the discussion I'd heard, including the daisy-haired witch's claim that she'd stolen the thorn-killer toxin from someone in the coven. Had she been telling the truth? If so, someone had died as a result of that very toxin... which made her a suspect.

"How did it end up in his drink, though?" I asked Ramsey. "That's what I don't get. There's nothing to tie any of those witches to Linus or his friend, is there?"

"No," he said. "That said, it's possible a connection will emerge in the course of the investigation."

"Or one of the witches at the coffee shop was trying to poison another and got the wrong target."

"That's a stretch, Robin," he said. "There's no proof."

"There might be," I went on. "The blond witch—their leader, I think—wasn't at the table when the others were discussing the toxin. She claimed she was going to the ladies' room, but she might have sneaked off to slip the poison into someone's drink instead. In fact, if she used magic, she wouldn't have needed to be anywhere near them."

"I can't base an accusation on speculation, Robin."

"I know, but it's worth looking into, isn't it—?"

Tansy interrupted by leaping onto my shoulder, startling me into dropping my coffee. The container burst open, soaking both me and Ramsey. Not to mention my uneaten sandwich—and the sceptre, which unleashed a flurry of sparks.

"Tansy!" I took a step back to avoid the sparks hitting any nearby tents and starting a fire.

"Sorry!" she squeaked. "I wanted to warn you—your mother and aunt are fighting again."

"I thought Aunt Shannon was in her own tent?" Shaking droplets of coffee off my sleeve, I hurried after my familiar, and Ramsey followed. He paid no attention to the stains on his pristine shirt as we approached the tent designated for the flower contest.

Inside, Mum stood nose-to-nose with her sister on the wooden stage at the front of the tent. Someone had decorated the place since I'd last been there; thorny stems intertwined up the pillars on either side of the stage, while tables had been arranged in a semicircle around the outskirts of the tent.

"Mother," Ramsey called to her.

To my surprise, she barely spared him a glance, her

attention fixed on her sister. "Ramsey, your aunt and I are having a chat."

"We certainly aren't." Aunt Shannon stepped off the stage, but she didn't lower her wand. "I've made it clear that there's nothing in the rules forbidding me from hosting my own event as part of the carnival."

"That's not what I'm here to talk about," said Ramsey. "I need to talk to the Wildwood Coven's leader alone, so I'd appreciate it if you gave us some privacy.

Ha. It was nice when my brother turned his attitude on other people for a change, especially someone who deserved it. Aunt Shannon's lips thinned, but since she'd already been on her way out of the tent, she gave a faint shrug and left the three of us alone.

Mum focused on me for the first time. "Why are you covered in coffee?"

"Because Tansy came running to warn me about you two trying to attack one another and accidentally knocked my coffee out of my hands." If I had been feeling petty, I might have asked her to buy me a replacement for the drink, not to mention for my sopping sandwich. "Also, Ramsey has news that might implicate certain contest entrants in that shifter's murder."

"Not necessarily," Ramsey cut in. "I found out that the shifter who was murdered on Saturday was poisoned using thorn-killer toxin, which is as deadly to humans as it is to plants. There's nothing to say *who* poisoned him, but Robin believes she heard a conversation—"

"I *did* overhear a conversation," I interjected, irked that he'd brush me off so easily. "The flower club members were discussing acquiring some thorn-killer toxin in order to cheat in the flower contest, and they seemed to think that it originally came from someone in our coven."

Mum sucked in a breath. "You think my sister was involved, Robin?"

"I can't prove anything, I know," I said. "She wasn't anywhere near the café, for a start, but if anyone in the coven would try to bend the rules, it's her."

"I can't consider an overheard conversation to be firm evidence," Ramsey said. "That said, the medical reports were clear that the shifter was poisoned to death using thorn-killer toxin, and that's the information I have to work with."

"I thought one of the flower club members was trying to poison another and got the wrong target," I added for Mum's benefit. "Yes, I know it's speculation, but you know Aunt Shannon has a good reason to try to get her youngest daughter into trouble, and it was Rowan who made the drink that poisoned the victim."

Mum's attention sharpened. "You didn't mention that earlier."

"You didn't ask." Mum's erratic behaviour when it came to her sister made me reluctant to throw fuel on the fire, though she'd been known to dismiss my theories concerning Aunt Shannon's scheming in the past. "I'd have thought she'd be too busy with the contest to bother messing with Rowan, but the timing seems suspect. Are any of the flower club's members around?"

"Not at the moment, no," Mum said. "That said, I would prefer to verify their innocence for the sake of tomorrow's contest."

"I can do that," Ramsey said. "First, though, I believe I'll have a word with your sister."

He left the tent, and I followed to avoid ending up alone with Mum.

Tansy joined me at the tent's opening and sheepishly

eyed my dripping clothes. "Sorry," she said. "I panicked when I saw them fighting."

"It's fine, but next time I have my hands full, maybe poke me in the ankle or something," I said to her. "Where'd Aunt Shannon go?"

"Back in her tent," she said. "She put some kind of defensive charm on the whole tent. When I tried to get in, a ward threw me a foot into the air."

"Is that allowed?" I directed that question to Ramsey, who'd begun to approach the bright-yellow tent himself. "If she stops the police from getting into her tent, it's breaking the law, technically."

"I intend to question her, not arrest her," he said. "You should wait here."

"I wasn't the one challenging her to a duel," I pointed out. "You can at least ask her to let you in and see what she says, right?"

As Ramsey approached, Aunt Shannon herself emerged from the tent, her face a mask of polite incredulity. "Can I help you? Did you know you're both covered in coffee?"

Like I could forget. I scraped together the last shreds of my dignity and met her smile with a hard stare.

"An accident," Ramsey said. "I'd like to have a word with you, if you don't mind, in private."

"That's unnecessary," she said. "If Lady Wildwood or the Head Witch has asked you to back up their claims about my actions being unlawful, let me assure you that I have the mayor's direct permission to be here."

"They didn't," Ramsey said. "I don't know if you're aware, but a local shifter was poisoned to death at the café on Saturday, and we found out that the substance used was a toxin known as thorn-killer, which is also deadly to plants."

"How tragic," she said. "Might I ask why you're telling

me this? Unless my sister has made yet another baseless assumption."

"This has nothing to do with Mum," I said to her. "We have reason to believe the thorn-killer toxin was obtained from someone within the Wildwood Coven itself. Know anything?"

Aunt Shannon gave a laugh. "Is this how the police conduct their investigations? What would entice you to believe I had anything to do with this except for your own paranoia?"

"I never suggested you were involved," said Ramsey. "Regardless of how the poisoner obtained the thorn-killer toxin, it resulted in someone's death, and it's my duty to get to the bottom of this. Since I've already spoken to everyone who was present in the café at the time, I'll be questioning all the entrants to the contest to find out where the killer might have obtained the poison."

"Including your mother, I'd hope."

Might have to wait for her to calm down first. Though it was beyond absurd to imagine Mum cheating in the flower contest *or* poisoning a stranger.

"Yes, including her," Ramsey answered. "Have you had access to thorn-killer toxin at any point recently? Have you or has anyone else you're aware of brewed or bought the substance?"

"No," she said. "Who exactly told you someone in the coven was responsible?"

Her gaze flickered to me, but I ignored her faked incredulity. "It's not rocket science. Most of the town's experts on potions and poisons are members of our coven."

"I am certainly not one of them," she said. "I wouldn't even know how to start brewing such a complex poison."

Complex, is it? I'd have to check for myself to see if she was telling the truth, but it seemed that she had no intention of giving anything away.

"I hope you're being honest," said Ramsey. "Thank you for cooperating with me."

"*I* hope this is the end of these absurd diversions." She gave me a dirty look that I thought was kind of undeserved. Did she think I'd called my brother here myself? Or did she somehow blame me for my mother's paranoia? Either way, I didn't appreciate it a bit, so I put on a scowl, somewhat dampened—literally—by the fact that I was covered in coffee.

"*Are* you going to question Mum?" I asked Ramsey when Aunt Shannon had disappeared into her tent. "Might be worth checking if the toxin really is that complex to brew— oh, and don't forget Vanessa has access to the coven's stores too. Aunt Shannon might have asked her to do it instead."

"She might," he said. "That said, I don't see why she would give the coven's supplies to a potential competitor in the contest."

"The witch who was boasting in the café claimed to have *stolen* the toxin. She wasn't given it."

"Stolen?"

"Yes, I told you." Had he even been paying attention? "I don't know if she was implying that she robbed the coven's stores or something else, but I thought you should know."

"So I see," he said. "Right. I'll talk to our mother and then the other contest entrants."

"Aren't you interested to see what Aunt Shannon is hiding in that tent?"

"Not especially."

Honestly. The guy had no sense of curiosity to speak of. "I'll let you know if Tansy manages to sneak in and get a peek."

I knew better than to listen in on his chat with Mum, especially if my name ended up being mentioned, since I assumed he was just humouring Aunt Shannon and that he didn't genuinely suspect our mother of brewing any thorn-killer toxin herself.

When he vanished into the flower tent, Tansy scampered over to me. "I can't even crawl underneath the back of the tent. She's determined not to let anyone in."

"I wonder if the mayor would tell us what she's up to if we asked." Most of the time, I forgot the town even *had* a mayor, because everyone knew the coven was really in charge. "He must know who I am."

Everyone did, unfortunately. Anonymity was a thing of the past, though I'd never really had it in the first place except in distant towns where nobody had heard of the Wildwood Coven. Still, the title of Head Witch came with another boatload of assumptions I hadn't asked for. Just look at how Dale Longfoot had reacted when I'd shown up at his house.

While Ramsey was talking to Mum, I bought a replacement for my wasted coffee and sandwich and fed crumbs to Tansy as we debated possible ways to unearth Aunt Shannon's tent's hidden contents.

"Whatever it is, it's legal," I added. "Unless she lied about consulting the mayor. Also, the shifters are more lenient about rules than the coven is."

"True," said Tansy. "That's why I like them better. Even the scary wolves."

"Jessica's kids aren't scary, are they?"

"No, not even when they forget not to grab my tail." She preened. "It *is* very pretty, so I can forgive them for it."

The tent flap lifted, and Ramsey caught sight of us standing outside. "You're still here?"

"Yes, because Mum told me to come here herself." I gestured at Aunt Shannon's tent. "Want to see if our aunt will let you in? Tansy and I were discussing talking to the mayor to find out if she did get permission to be here."

"No," he said bluntly. "I meant it when I said I have to question the rest of the contest entrants. I know the ones at the café left before the murder took place..."

"Doesn't mean they weren't involved," I said. "In fact, they might even still have the thorn-killer toxin. Even if not, the contest is tomorrow, and we'll find out pretty quickly if anyone's been cheating."

"We will," he said. "Though I'd prefer to have answers before then."

"Me too." I crouched beside Tansy. "Can you stay here and keep an eye on those two in case they start another fight?"

Ramsey cleared his throat. "You aren't coming, Robin."

I straightened upright. "You didn't think I was going to stay behind while you talked to the flower club members, did you?"

"Are we referring to the same flower club that you announced as the 'flour cub' when you were an apprentice?"

Of course *he* remembered that. My face burned at the memory, but I couldn't let a little embarrassment put me off getting to the bottom of their potential involvement in the murder. "I was also *in* the coffee shop when they were publicly bragging, and I can give you a description of everyone involved."

"Can you, now?" he said. "Their leader is called Araminta. I'm familiar with her."

"She was the blonde," I recalled. "She also wasn't involved in the cheating discussion, but she was bragging about her rhododendrons a fair bit. Might be worth talking to her."

Her attitude towards the staff at the café had left much to be desired, but if she was unaware of the cheating that might be taking place right under her nose, it might be a wise idea to get her on our side.

Let's see what she has to say.

7

———————

Firstly, I insisted on stopping at home to change out of my coffee-soaked clothes, and Ramsey reluctantly did the same, mostly so we'd make a slightly better impression on the head of the flower club. Given the way she'd treated the staff at the coffee shop, I wasn't sure if I'd have any more luck with her than I would with the daisy-haired witch who viewed me with such disdain, but she hadn't said anything unpleasant about me behind my back the way the others had. She might even have known my grandmother, given that they were around the same age and had doubtless entered many of the same contests.

Ramsey and I left the house and walked down the main street through the middle of town. There seemed to be fewer people around than usual, though the locals might have started to gravitate towards the carnival by now. Which reminded me: we had a couple of hours at most until the first visitors from outside of Wildwood Heath would start arriving, so I'd need to ensure I got back to the field in good time if I wanted to avoid another spat with my mother. I only hoped she and Aunt Shannon would stay well away from one another.

In an attempt to take my mind off the mental image of my mother and aunt duelling in full view of the public, I asked my brother if he'd made any progress in other areas of the investigation.

"You mean questioning suspects?" he asked. "No, I haven't. I did speak to the employer of both Linus Tooley and Dale Longfoot, but he claimed not to have known anything about their rivalry."

"Right. Linus had just been promoted," I recalled. "Dale had wanted the position and got annoyed at his bragging. Is his boss going to hire someone else instead?"

"He said the office was still adjusting to the shock of losing Linus and that he hasn't made a decision yet."

"Hmm. It'd be interesting if Dale ended up getting the job after all, wouldn't it?"

"No."

I blinked at his abrupt tone. "I'm not saying Dale engineered the situation on purpose, and I know we're supposed to be talking to the flower club witches, but I assumed you'd kept his name on the suspect list. Is there anyone else who might have decided to swipe a deadly toxin from the witches to poison him?"

"There's also an ex-boyfriend, but he wasn't anywhere near the café at the time," Ramsey said. "It's unlikely that the person responsible wasn't present at the time."

"That or they just left." Which brought us back to the flower club again. "Where do the flower club members live?"

"Araminta, their leader, lives in Acacia Avenue," he said. "They usually hold their meetings at her house, though they've recently taken to having weekly informal gatherings at the coffee shop as well."

"Since when were you an expert on the flower club?"

"Hardly an expert," he responded. "I've worked with the public here in Wildwood Heath for a long time, however, and one tends to pick up a few things."

I didn't appreciate the implication that my absence from town for the past few years worked against me. Not only was I fully aware already, but I'd hardly expected to need to know the intricacies of the flower club's meeting schedule at any point during my tenure as Head Witch.

Upon catching sight of my irritated expression, he added, "The flower club has been regularly meeting for longer than either of us have been alive, and I don't think they've changed up their schedule at all in that time."

"Sticklers for tradition?" I should have figured. "Are they coven members?"

"They've all retired from official duties, I believe," he said. "That said, I believe most of them were formerly employed by the Wildwood Coven."

My mouth parted. Daisy Hair hadn't seemed to have much respect for the coven—or for me, anyway—though since Mum *was* a potential rival in the flower contest, they might have put those former loyalties aside. "Aren't there any younger members who aren't retired?"

"They're quite stringent with their membership requirements."

"Meaning they haven't taken on anyone new in half a century?" I shook my head. "If they've retired from all coven-related activities, I guess they made an exception for the flower contest."

"Correct." Ramsey led the way into a picturesque street lined with cosy-looking bungalows. Bright flowers bloomed in the gardens to the extent that it was tricky to tell which house belonged to their leader.

"Guess nobody here has pollen allergies," I remarked, following him to a door patterned with painted rhododendrons.

When he knocked on the door, the blond witch from the previous day answered, carrying a large flowerpot in her arms.

"Can I help you?" Araminta's gaze landed on the sceptre in my hand. "Head Witch. To what do I owe the pleasure?"

"Ah, I'm not here as Head Witch." I indicated my brother. "I'm here with the police."

"The police?" Araminta squinted at Ramsey's neat badge. "Now, what do the police want here in our quiet little neighbourhood?"

"I'm here to talk to all the entrants of tomorrow's flower contest," Ramsey said. "May I come in and ask some questions?"

"Yes, I suppose you may." She stepped back to allow us to enter a living room that contained more flowers than furniture and whose walls were transparent, like a greenhouse. Bright plants bloomed in pots on shelves, sofas, and tables, and the perfumed scent was enough to make me screw up my eyes. So was the glaringly bright light on the ceiling, which appeared to be a spell to mimic the sun's rays. She couldn't possibly be entering all of these in the contest, could she?

"My apologies for not offering you a seat," she said. "I'm keeping my collection indoors to ensure my best specimens are safe for tomorrow's contest. I wouldn't want anything to go wrong so close to the big event."

"Do you have reason to believe it might?" Ramsey enquired.

"Is this a police interrogation?" Araminta sounded intrigued. "I haven't been involved in one of those in a while."

Does she mean recently? I couldn't tell how old she was, since the blond hair was either a wig or dyed, and her face was oddly smooth, suggesting she was using a spell or potion to make her features appear more youthful. When she caught me watching her, she cocked one dyed brow as if to say, *What're you looking at?*

"Then I hope you can tell me if anyone in your club has been involved in illicit activities," said Ramsey. "We've recently discovered that the substance known as thorn-killer toxin is circulating in town, which is deadly to both plants and humans."

"I've heard of the stuff, yes," she said. "You won't find any of that in here, I can assure you."

"Someone was poisoned to death using the same substance," Ramsey went on. "They died in the same café where your group spent Saturday morning, shortly after you left, and the subject of thorn-killer toxin was mentioned among your group."

"Who told you we were there?" she huffed. "Can't we go to a coffee shop without people poking their noses into our business?"

She and the others had been airing their business for the whole world to hear, but I decided not to point that out. I'd been lucky they hadn't seen me eavesdropping on them.

"The café's owner told me you've recently taken to meeting up there on Saturdays," he said. "It's not the contents of your meetings that concern me, but there seems little reason for anyone to procure thorn-killer toxin if not to use it."

"So you're accusing someone in my group of committing murder?"

"No," said Ramsey. "I am not. That said, I'd like to find out where the thorn-killer toxin is currently located so that I can be sure that it does no harm to anyone else. If you can point me to anyone, whether they are a member of your club or not, who would have reason to interfere in the contest, I'd be grateful."

"Seems to me that you're confusing two completely different crimes," Araminta said. "Why would anyone who had their hands on thorn-killer toxin carry it around in public, much less use it to murder a person and not a plant?"

To brag about it to their friends. But she hadn't actively been involved in that conversation, and if I pointed that out, I'd have to admit I'd been listening. Did I want to risk the backlash? She might not even know about her fellow flower club members' scheming, though I had my doubts that she'd have no awareness of what was going on right under her nose.

"I haven't a clue," I told her. "The killer certainly got hold of it somehow, and we can't discount the possibility that it was originally intended to be used on someone's plants."

"Well, I know nothing of such things," she said sniffily. "All I do is run my flower club and stay out of trouble, which ought to be enough to spare me from being visited by the police."

"Someone has died," Ramsey said sternly, not falling for her innocent act. "With the contest tomorrow and most of the townspeople expected to be in attendance, it's vital that we find where the poison is located so it doesn't harm anyone else. If we unearth any potential sabotage in the contest in the process, it'll work out in your favour, won't it?"

"If you're implying that I desire to profit from my own members' suffering, you're mistaken," she said. "I'd like nothing more than to see my fellow witches all furnished with the prizes they deserve, but I assume your coven leader expects to take the top prize once again."

"You don't mind if I search your property, then?" Ramsey asked.

"You may, but you'd better not damage any of my flowers."

That was a tall order given the sheer number of them. The odds of us finding any flower-killing toxins in here were incredibly low, but I couldn't exactly leave Ramsey to deal with it alone. While I was glad her house had only one floor to search, plant pots and bags of soil blocked the doors to every cupboard and covered every surface. A glance out the back window confirmed her back garden was equally well-tended.

"How are we supposed to find anything in here?" I asked him in an undertone. "What does thorn-killer toxin even look like? Even if it has a distinct scent, this place smells like a perfume shop."

"It'll be in a heavily sealed container," he said. "It's a clear liquid and is potent enough that only a drop would suffice."

"To kill a plant. Or person." I grimaced. "The trouble is, the person who had it has had enough time to dispose of the evidence by now."

Araminta watched with a scowl as we searched as thoroughly as we could manage, though even if the toxin had been in a sealed container, Araminta might not have wanted to risk causing damage to her plants by keeping it inside her house. After checking each room, Ramsey and I returned to the living room.

"I apologise for the inconvenience, Araminta," he said. "I'll come back if I have any more questions."

"I sincerely hope that won't be necessary." Her gaze went to me. "I have to admit this isn't how I expected to meet the new Head Witch, especially given that her predecessor was a close friend to the flower club."

What did she expect me to say to that? My lack of interest in flowers aside, I would have thought the implied age limit on membership to the flower club would have rendered me unqualified to sign up. Besides, the idea of spending any more time with her than I already had to was about as appealing as gargling thorn-killer toxin.

"My apologies," I said in the tone Mum used when forced to interact politely with her sister. "I've had a rather busy start to my tenure as Head Witch."

"No doubt," she said. "Of course, Willow Wildwood was a hard act to follow, and no doubt the coven greatly misses her expertise."

Ouch. No doubt she didn't know that my grandmother was currently haunting my office, and I had no intention of enlightening her on the subject. "Every Head Witch is different."

"Yes, I don't doubt that," she said. "We attended her funeral ourselves, and it would have been nice to have the successor's blessing, but I understand it was a difficult time for your family."

Considering I hadn't even known I'd end up being Head Witch at the time and neither had anyone else, it was lucky I'd been there at all, but I didn't need to burn any more bridges today by refusing to give my blessing to a group that might be hiding a murderer.

"Thank you for your time," Ramsey said, coming to my rescue. "We should leave."

"It was a pleasure meeting you," I added.

She didn't call me out on the lie, nor did she return the sentiment before we left the house.

"Everything I own is going to smell like flowers for a week," I remarked to Ramsey when the door closed behind us. "Though at least we're no longer covered in cheap instant coffee."

Ramsey apparently didn't consider that as much of a silver lining as I did. He simply grunted and walked ahead of me as if the lack of answers had put him in a bad mood. He hadn't expected to find the thorn-killer toxin hidden in plain sight, had he?

"Did you expect a confession?" I asked him. "For the record, she wasn't involved in that conversation I overheard. The witch I want to speak to is the one with daisies in her hair."

"I can't identify someone from a description that vague, Robin."

"I wasn't going to get any closer in case she recognised me," I told him. "She was already talking about me behind my back. Also, I'm surprised Grandma was friendly with their group if they were rivals in the flower contest."

"It's only once a year," he reminded me. "The rest of the time, they probably traded tips on how to keep their flowers in bloom. As for the person you overheard in the café—even if she claimed to have the thorn-killer toxin at the time, she might not currently have it in her hands."

"That would be too simple, huh?" She might not have been responsible for poisoning the victim, either, but since she was the one who claimed the coven had had the thorn-killer toxin to begin with, she was still at the top of my suspect list. "If nobody will admit to anything, the truth might be exposed at the contest."

"True," Ramsey said. "You'll be helping with the judging, won't you? You can expose the cheater in no time."

"Wait, I'm not a judge," I said. "Family members aren't allowed to. Conflict of interest."

Also, I didn't know anything about flowers, which seemed a minimum requirement to say the least.

"I didn't say you had to judge the contest itself, but we need someone to keep an eye out," he said. "Your sceptre ought to be more than capable of detecting any potential sabotage."

"Hang on a second," I protested. "Talk to Mum before you volunteer me for anything else without asking her."

"I'll be surprised if she hasn't already thought of this," he said. "If there's a toxin hidden among the plants that's too subtle to be detected by a wand, your sceptre would certainly be able to expose it."

Unfortunately, he was right. Not that I'd ever tried to cast a spell like that using my sceptre before. "We'll see if Mum agrees. Are you heading back to the carnival now? Or talking to the other flower club members?"

"There are thirty listed members," he said. "Some of them aren't even entering the contest. Knocking on doors until we find the right person is hardly the most efficient method of tracking down the witch you overheard."

He might have a point there. "Then what else will you do?"

"I'll talk to the owner of the café again," he said. "See if he or any of the other baristas have information on the flower club witches who were present on Saturday."

"Including Rowan?" I guessed. "You know, if you want to go straight to the source, it'd save time if you searched her mother's house instead. Or her office. I'd bet you'd find traces of that thorn-killer toxin if not the stuff itself."

"I can't break into her property based on a hunch," he said. "She's too clever to have hidden the proof in plain sight, if it exists, and she must know she'd instantly become a suspect if anything happened to our mother's flowers."

I shuddered. "Yeah, I don't really want to imagine what Mum would do to her. Honestly, that tent of hers is suspect enough."

She wouldn't have hidden the thorn-killer toxin in *there*, though, right?

Ramsey gave me a sideways look. "Regardless, our aunt hasn't been anywhere near the coffee shop in the time since the murder."

"How do you know?" The certainty I'd heard in his voice gave me pause. "You've been watching the café?"

"Not me," he said. "My familiar. He's there right now, in fact."

"You sent Prickles to watch the place?" I asked. "I thought you didn't believe my aunt was involved."

"No, but it's useful to have eyes in more than one place," he said. "Even if our aunt declined to show up to taunt her daughter, I thought the killer might return to the scene of the crime."

"You did?" I wasn't about to complain about the added security, especially with my own familiar occupied with keeping my mother and aunt from starting a public duel. "I think our aunt's too busy setting up her tent at the carnival to pester Rowan. That makes this an ideal time to search her office, if you ask me."

He shook his head. "I need to inform the café's owner that we've identified the poison used on the victim while I'm here. I'm also going to search the premises in case the killer left any clues behind."

Unlikely, if they hadn't already shown up, but I could always pay a sneaky visit to Aunt Shannon's office myself. Or Tansy could. "Let me know how it goes. I should head back before Mum comes looking for me."

Or worse, before she and Aunt Shannon got into another fight. Though at least then I might be able to find a way into Shannon's tent while she was distracted.

And if it isn't her? Who else in the coven might be trying to interfere in the contest?

8

———

I returned to the carnival to find my mother in consultation with the contest's judges outside the tent. At least she wasn't fighting her sister, but she didn't appear to have noticed I'd been gone.

Tansy popped up at my side. "Aunt Shannon's still hiding in her tent, but I can't get in. I've tried everything."

From the mud all over her paws, I guessed she'd been trying to dig her way in. "I have a better idea. Want to sneak into her office instead while she's not around?"

"Really?" She sat straight upright, her eyes gleaming with interest. "Why?"

"Wash your paws first," I advised her. "If there's proof that Aunt Shannon's been brewing up thorn-killer toxin, it'll be in her office."

"Shouldn't that be Ramsey's job?"

"He's at the café, talking to the owner," I explained. "Might be searching the premises too."

"Including Rowan's flat?"

"I hope *not*." It'd be just like Ramsey to leave no stone unturned, though. I should have guessed.

"I can go and check," Tansy offered. "I'd prefer not to go to your aunt's office alone in case that ghastly magpie comes after me."

"Yeah... I'm surprised Mum didn't get mad at me for leaving." I kept my voice low. "All right, you should check up on Rowan. I think she could use the moral support."

"My pleasure." Tansy scurried away, and I tried to peer into Aunt Shannon's tent without any luck. I could probably lift whatever defences she'd put up if I used the sceptre, but that might have the side effect of undoing the other necessary defences around the field itself. We had less than an hour before the event opened to the public, so I didn't dare take the risk.

When Mum finished chatting to the judges, she spotted me standing outside the tent. "Robin, don't stand there looking gormless. Go back to the office."

"I thought I was supposed to oversee the carnival's official opening," I reminded her, though that had admittedly been prior to Aunt Shannon's shenanigans. "Or find out what's going on here." I gestured at the new tent, which remained as impenetrable as ever.

"Leave *that* to me." Her nostrils flared. "Where is your brother?"

"Talking to the staff at the café," I answered. "He's searching the place for thorn-killer toxin, but I think it's unlikely he'll find any there. It's more likely to be in the office of whoever brewed it. Right?"

I'd used the word "office" pointedly, but she didn't take the bait. "Then let him get on with it, Robin. I did tell you not to concern yourself with the investigation, didn't I?"

"The investigation led right here, to the contest." I gestured at the field. "Which reminds me—what plans did you have in place to detect cheating tomorrow?"

"Everyone will hand in their wands before entering the tent, and no familiars will be permitted inside," she said. "The judges will perform spells to detect any hidden sabotage unless you'd like to volunteer to do so yourself."

"Uh... well, that's what Ramsey suggested," I said. "But I haven't practised that spell with the sceptre..."

"Then ask your grandmother to teach you," said Mum, waving a dismissive hand at me. "Go on."

So much for being allowed to stay at the carnival. Her change in mood gave me whiplash, though it was understandable that she'd want to keep an eye on her sister herself, and there was little I could do to help the judges plan how to decide whose flowers were the most impressive.

I followed the woodland path alone, wondering if I ought to go ahead with my original plan to search Aunt Shannon's office. I'd need to wait for my familiar first, so I made for the witches' headquarters, assuming Chloe was right where I'd left her in my office.

I'd barely entered my own office when Tansy came skidding into the room and jumped onto my desk, scattering pens everywhere.

"They've arrested her!" she squeaked.

"Arrested who?" My heart lurched. "Not Rowan?"

"They found the thorn-killer toxin in her flat!"

"What?" I looked to Chloe, who sat at her desk with her mouth slightly open. "Uh—Chloe—"

"I'll tell the other witches where you've gone if anyone asks, don't worry," said Chloe. "You go and help your cousin."

"Thanks. I owe you one." I ran out of the office on Tansy's heels, glad Mum wasn't in the building to waylay me and demand I stay put.

Rowan. I ran down the road and scarcely stopped to

breathe until I saw the police gathering outside the café. A pale-faced Rowan stood flanked by two officers.

Her eyes bulged when she saw me. "Robin, they found the thorn-killer toxin in my cupboard, but I swear I have no idea how it got there."

"That's what you'd say whether you were guilty or not, isn't it?" said one of the officers in a nasty tone of voice. "It can't have flown in, can it?"

It might have. If it'd been in the claws of a certain magpie, anyway.

"Have you forgotten magic is a thing?" I asked the officers. "Also, what possible reason would Rowan have to store a toxin that's deadly to plants in her flat? She keeps pet tarantulas whose safety she wouldn't want to risk, and she's not even entering the flower contest herself."

"If we find proof to the contrary, we'll gladly set her free." The words came from Ramsey, who stepped out of the café with Rowan's boss behind him. Mal looked almost as stunned as Rowan herself did.

"You know as well as I do that this is a setup," I said to Ramsey and his fellow officers. "Rowan is an easy target, that's all, and you're playing into the hands of the person who really killed Linus if you arrest her instead of them."

"It's a precautionary measure," Ramsey said in stern tones. "Until we find out how that toxin got into her flat."

I noticed belatedly that Tansy had disappeared; when I looked up, I saw her fluffy tail near Rowan's open window.

"Was that window always open?" I asked the officers. "Because if not, then it'd be easy for someone to have got inside while Rowan was at work downstairs."

Or would it? I'd momentarily forgotten Rowan had set up a magpie-proof net on the roof to prevent her mother's familiar from getting too close to her room. I tilted my head back to look at Tansy, who sniffed the window a couple of times before scooting back down the drainpipe and hopping onto my shoulder.

I shivered as her fluffy tail tickled my ear. "The net's still up there. Nobody climbed in."

No. That would be too easy.

"It's been two days since the murder," Ramsey said, ignoring our quiet exchange. "That's long enough for someone to have planted the toxin in Rowan's flat, true, but there's no proof it wasn't Rowan herself. Rowan will have the chance to give her account of events in due time."

My heart seized, but the officers ignored my protests and led Rowan away from the café ahead of my brother. Ramsey himself looked back at me, a hint of regret in his expression, before walking away.

"She didn't do this." I approached Mal, silently pleading with the universe not to take away everything my cousin had worked for. "She didn't."

"I know she didn't." He heaved a sigh. "I don't understand how that poison got into her flat though, and I won't deny it looks bad for her."

"Like I said, she was a convenient target," I said. "Not just because she lives above the café but because she's connected to the coven even if she has no plans to enter that flower contest."

"Is this all really about a contest, though?" he queried. "That toxin is deadly to more than just plants."

"Yeah... some people really like to win." I debated inwardly for a moment. I'd never really discussed the subject of Rowan's family with Mal before—never had an actual conversation with him at all, in fact—and I'd been reluctant to enlighten him on the depths of Aunt Shannon's pettiness in case he decided that housing a member of her family was more trouble than it was worth. "I saw the flower club has been using your café as a meeting spot. They're entering the contest."

"Them?" he said. "They're rude to my staff, which doesn't sit right with me, but I can't see any of them committing murder."

"You can't deny it's more likely to be one of them than Rowan," I persisted. "Do you know the name of the one with daisies in her hair?"

"No, I'm afraid I don't," he said. "Sorry, Head Witch, but I have to go. Since I'm going to be down a worker for the time being, the rest of my staff need to know about their shifts changing."

"Wait." I didn't quite know what I was going to say, but the idea of leaving Rowan to her fate was repellent. "Uh— what about her familiar? She has tarantulas upstairs... someone needs to feed them or keep an eye on them."

"I can do it myself, since I have the key," he said. "Don't worry. They'll be fine."

That was something, at least, but who'd got into her flat to plant the so-called evidence to begin with? Had the magpie found a way past the net on the window, or had some determined individual used magic to break in through the door?

As he walked back into the café, I couldn't shake the feeling that I'd made things worse for Rowan instead of better by talking to her boss, but I knew I'd have regretted it if I hadn't at least tried to help her.

Tansy and I looked at one another in mutual despair.

"This won't stand," she said, her tail sticking up in indignation. "If your aunt did this, we'll make her pay for it."

"Yeah." I dragged my gaze away from the café. "We will."

As luck would have it, Aunt Shannon was back at her office when we got back to the witches' headquarters, and while I might have seized on the opportunity to sneak a look into her tent, Tansy informed me that her magpie was keeping a close watch on the opening. Foiled again.

Resigned, I sat down to an entirely unproductive afternoon at the office and forgot all about my mother's request to ask my grandmother for lessons in using detecting spells with the sceptre until Grandma herself appeared behind my desk.

"What is that?" She indicated my laptop screen, which showed a screensaver of a selection of adorable baby Pokémon running in circles.

"Correspondence." I dragged up the letter I was supposed to be working on, addressed to some important individual who had no idea that I typed my responses on my laptop and then handed them off to Chloe to write out by hand. My own handwriting was atrocious, and my spelling was worse, so it was the best way to ensure everyone was happy... except my mother, who'd tutted in disapproval when she found out.

In any case, I had trouble caring about any of this when my cousin was sitting in a jail cell for a crime she'd never committed.

"Looks like a mess to me," Grandma commented.

I flushed, looking down at my computer screen, on which I'd written a single line and managed to misspell half the words even with the autocorrect function switched on. "Grandma, did you know one of your grandchildren has been arrested?"

"Which one? Ramsey?"

"No, Ramsey's the one who did the arresting. It's Rowan." I rested my head in my hands. "And I'm pretty sure it's my fault."

My chair yanked itself out from underneath me, causing me to crash to the floor. I yelped, raising my head. "What the hell, Grandma?"

"No moping on the job."

"Ow." I got to my feet, rubbing my back. "That was uncalled for."

"But deserved." She hovered beside my desk, unimpressed. "You have work to do."

"It's hardly more important than my cousin being in jail." I gingerly sat down again, watching her out of the corner of my eye as I did so. "I could be doing something useful, like finding out which coven member has been supplying the flower club with thorn-killer toxin so I can find out who planted it in Rowan's room."

"Thorn-killer toxin?" Grandma echoed. "I wouldn't touch that stuff. It's—"

"Deadly to plants and humans, I know," I interjected. "Someone used it to commit murder the other day and then planted the evidence on Rowan."

"Who?" she asked. "Are you *sure* your cousin wasn't involved herself?"

I was starting to regret bringing up the subject. "Rowan has literally no reason to obtain plant-killing poison. Unlike, say, anyone who's planning on entering the flower contest tomorrow."

"It's that time of year already?"

"What planet have you been on?"

"The afterworld, and I'll thank you to treat me with a little more respect." Grandma's expression turned pensive. "I miss the flower contest. Do you think they'll let me attend?"

"Can you travel that far?" As far as we knew, she could just about reach our house but no further. Privately, I was glad her mayhem was confined to the office. I didn't need her tailing me on my walks through the forest as well as rearranging my desk. "If so, you're welcome to come and watch, but I'd prefer to find out who's trading in thorn-killer toxin first. Especially as they might have got it from someone in the coven."

"That stuff isn't easy to brew," Grandma said. "Except perhaps for the Henbane Coven."

"The Henbanes?" The Wildwood Coven's main rival was a shadow of its former self with its leader and its most important members currently jailed for plotting against me, but the mere mention of the name put my nerves on edge. "You don't think they're involved? Is there anyone left who might be entering the contest?"

"They're better at killing plants than growing them." Grandma chuckled darkly to herself.

That sounded about right. "Where else might someone obtain thorn-killer?"

"If they bought it, they must have intended to use it," she said. "Expensive stuff, that."

Wait. "Have the Henbanes brewed thorn-killer toxin in the past, do you know?"

"I haven't the faintest idea," Grandma said. "I always thought the Henbanes could have made a fortune selling their poisons if they hadn't been more interested in hoarding them all for their own use."

My mouth parted. If she was telling the truth, the person who had the thorn-killer toxin might not have brewed it at all... which blew any chance we might have had of finding proof in a house or office.

Chloe cleared her throat. "Ah—sorry, Robin, I don't

know if you forgot, but your mother wanted me to remind you to practise using the sceptre to cast a detecting charm."

"I did forget." I suppressed a groan. "Grandma, my mum wants you to teach me to use detection charms so I can find out if anyone's smuggling any dodgy items into the contest tomorrow."

"Does she now?" she said. "Then I must oblige."

Oh, joy.

I LEFT the office bruised and aching and not at all looking forward to an evening of dealing with Mum's last-minute angst as she prepared for the contest tomorrow. At least Piper would be there to help, so we'd suffer together, and I doubted that a small thing like my cousin being arrested would distract my mother from the competition.

When I arrived home, I found both Mum and Piper were already in the back garden. Mum had picked out the best of the rosebushes and set them aside in their pots, where they bloomed brightly in shades of pink and red and white. Not a stem or petal was out of place despite the birds crowding the feeder. Generally, even the wildlife knew better than to trespass in the coven leader's flowerbeds, and Horace, her familiar, was the only animal even allowed into the greenhouses.

"Rowan's been arrested," I told them both. "I don't know if you heard."

"I did," said Mum. "Have you been practising the detection spell?"

She had a one-track mind. "Yes. I've got it down. Despite, you know, my cousin being in *jail.*"

Granted, there were very few ways to mess up a detection spell, and even if I did manage to screw up, the odds were low that I'd accidentally set anything on fire. *Low bar there, Robin.*

"Good," she said. "Don't touch anything."

And she returned to the house, leaving me blinking after her. Was she not even going to comment on her niece's arrest? I knew she didn't want to be distracted, but it was obvious she was going to win the contest, and the potential saboteur might be the same person who'd framed my cousin.

Piper sidled over to me. "I'm sorry about Rowan."

"So am I, believe me," I said. "I wish I knew who planted that toxin in her room."

"You don't think it was your aunt, do you?"

"I honestly don't know," I admitted. "I don't think she was responsible for the actual poisoning incident, but she might have wanted to dispose of the evidence if she thought it might be traced back to her."

"Your mum still wants you to use detection spells at the contest, though?"

"We arranged that before the thorn-killer toxin showed up at Rowan's, but there are other ways to cheat in the contest." I gloomily surveyed the various pots and flowerbeds. "I don't think even Aunt Shannon would dare to try to target Mum's plants. I also don't know why she'd bother, since everyone knows Mum will win."

"True." Her forehead wrinkled. "Was she trying to take out the minor competition in case one of them snagged second or third place?"

"Honestly, I doubt it," I said. "Not least because she wasn't anywhere near the café at the time, though that doesn't mean she had no hand in giving the thorn-killer toxin to the person who did it. Whether she knew what they'd do with it is debatable, but she has an interest in making Rowan's life difficult."

"That's true," she said. "The police seem to be lacking in hard evidence, though. If this started out as a spat over the flower contest, how'd a shifter end up being poisoned to death?"

"My theory was that someone from that flower club was trying to poison their rival and got the wrong target," I said. "The café was so crowded that day that I can see how that might have happened, but Ramsey doesn't believe me."

"He arrested your cousin instead?" She gave a low whistle. "I know he can be intense, but that doesn't sound like your brother."

"He wasn't happy with the situation, but they found the poison in her flat," I said. "Never mind that there was no good reason for it to be there. She has nothing to do with the contest, after all, but they can't go against the evidence unless they find proof it was planted."

"Awful," she said. "I bet that magpie flew in through the window."

"We put a net on the window, remember?" I told her. "Also, my brother's familiar has been keeping an eye on the café ever since the murder, if you can believe it, and he hasn't seen Aunt Shannon or her familiar anywhere near the place."

"Your brother was watching out for Rowan? Really?"

"Nah, he claimed he wanted to see if the killer returned to the scene of the crime."

"Well, that's nonsense," said Piper. "If you ask me, he knew it would upset you if she got into trouble, and he wanted to avoid it."

"If so, then he failed." I shook my head. "I don't think that's it. He didn't want Rowan to be arrested, true, but mostly because of the hit to our family's reputation. And probably because it'd distract me from my duties as Head Witch."

"I doubt that's all, Robin," Piper said. "He cares about you, but he's like your mum. Neither of them can express their feelings in words."

"Whereas I'm like my dad and wear my heart on my sleeve. I know."

I knew my brother cared about me despite how he acted sometimes, but the fact remained that he'd arrested Rowan, and now I was stuck dealing with this ridiculous contest instead of helping him find the person who'd framed my cousin.

Admittedly, most of the suspects would be *at* the contest, so if I caught them out first thing tomorrow, Rowan would be out of jail before word of her arrest had time to spread throughout the town.

"Speaking of your dad, has Ramsey talked to him?" asked Piper.

"Not since he questioned him about the murder," I said. "Poor guy. Meaning Dad, not Ramsey."

"Your family doesn't do grudges by halves, do they?" she remarked. "Ah... there's your mum. I should talk with her about her plans for transporting the flowers to the carnival tomorrow."

"Good luck." I didn't need to involve myself in that one, so I looked for an escape route and spotted Tansy beginning one of her ill-advised attempts to climb the bird feeder. As I caught up to her, my gaze fell on Aunt Shannon's house on the other side of the fence.

Did Aunt Shannon know her daughter was in jail? I sincerely doubted she'd care either way, and I wouldn't stoop to asking her directly. The contest was first thing tomorrow, though, so I'd have to face her soon enough.

"Hey, Tansy." I beckoned her down from the bird feeder. "Can you see my aunt anywhere in her garden?"

"Nope," she said. "I bet she's back at the carnival."

"With her mysterious tent." I'd had about enough of all the secrecy. "Want to see if my newly mastered detection spell picks up anything over there?"

Tansy waved her tail in enthusiasm. "I like the way you think."

9

———

Using my sceptre to sneakily cast spells on my aunt's property was not behaviour becoming of a Head Witch, I knew, and while Mum always said that my job was twenty-four hours a day, seven days a week and that I was still Head Witch even when asleep, that didn't mean I had to act the part all the time.

Besides, wasn't it also my job to detect any potential sabotage in the flower contest? Aunt Shannon might have claimed to have the mayor's permission to set up her tent, but for all I knew, she'd picked its location precisely because it was right next to the contest.

As we walked through the garden, Tansy tried to climb the fence separating my mother's house from Aunt Shannon's and instantly slid off again. The fence had been enhanced with a ward. That was new.

"She's not taking any chances, then," I remarked. "Interesting. I wonder if she left her flowers unsupervised while she's setting up her tent."

I had zero interest in messing with my aunt's garden, but I couldn't suppress a twinge of curiosity as to what had so occupied her attention that she'd willingly left her precious contest entries out of her sight on the eve of the event.

Also, let's face it—I was willing to seize on any possible evidence that my aunt might have left out in the open that might spare her daughter from a jail sentence.

Tansy and I kept our eyes open for signs of anyone in the garden—or in the sky—as we walked alongside the fence. I wasn't quite tall enough to see over it, and no matter which spot Tansy picked to climb, she simply slid straight back down to earth.

"I saw the magpie." Shedding bits of cut grass from her fur, she scampered back to my side. "Myrtle's guarding the greenhouse."

"Makes sense that she wouldn't leave her plants unattended." I gave up on the idea of going into her garden and house to search for evidence, though it'd been a long shot. If she'd once had the thorn-killer toxin, it would be long gone by now. As for how she'd obtained it? If Grandma had been right when she'd claimed that it was expensive to buy and tricky to brew—except allegedly for the Henbane Coven— then I was out of ideas.

Tansy and I followed the fence until we came to the back gate, which opened onto the woodland path. On my right stood the identical back gate to Aunt Shannon's house, which I tried to peer over, but the overgrown part of the back garden masked my view of anything else except the house. It certainly didn't look as if anyone had applied any plant-killing toxins, but she'd know better than to test them on her own garden.

"Be careful," I warned Tansy when she tried to climb the gate and promptly tumbled off. At least my aunt hadn't attached any sticky traps this time around, but it looked as if she'd covered her entire property in the same repelling charms that she'd used on her tent. "Leave it. We'll go to the carnival."

Tansy caught her balance, flicking dirt and bits of leaf everywhere, and then scaled a tree to peer over the back gate into Aunt Shannon's garden. "Looks the same as usual. You know, if that magpie is the only defence in front of the greenhouse..."

"There are probably magical alarms set to go off if anyone messes with her security spells," I pointed out. "C'mon. We need to get to the field before Mum figures out what we're up to."

In theory, I was allowed to do as I wanted to in my free time, but Mum's behaviour had been so erratic recently that I didn't want to inadvertently provoke another argument.

Tansy and I followed the woodland trail until we neared the field, at which point I pulled out my wand and cast an unseen spell on both of us so Aunt Shannon wouldn't see me approaching her tent.

"Why not use the sceptre?" It was weird to hear Tansy's voice coming out of nowhere, thanks to the spell keeping her hidden.

"Because I don't want to overdo it," I said. "Knowing my luck, it'd turn me permanently invisible."

Tansy snickered. "Wouldn't that be fun? Imagine how confused the pigeons would be if an invisible squirrel kept stealing their food."

"It'd get old fast; I guarantee it," I told her. "Also, you should give the poor pigeons a break."

An unseen spell was one of the more basic charms, and it wouldn't hold up under close scrutiny, but it'd do the job.

When we reached Aunt Shannon's tent, I lifted my sceptre and cast the spell I'd spent the afternoon practising under Grandma's watchful eye. The detection charm shimmered in the air for an instant, but all it picked up on was a basic security spell around the tent's boundaries, which I already knew about.

"Dammit," I muttered. "I was so sure I'd catch her in the act."

The act of *what,* exactly, was debatable, but if she was hiding anything illegal, my sceptre would have picked up on it. I paced around the back of the tent and tried another detection charm, but the results were the same.

"You can undo her security, right?" Tansy asked.

"Yeah... but not with the sceptre. I can't take the risk." The carnival wasn't at its full capacity yet, but doors had officially opened to visitors from outside of Wildwood Heath, and the clamour of excited voices drifted over from the other side of the field.

I reached for my wand instead and cast a charm to unravel any spells on the back of the tent, not expecting it to work. The sceptre amplified my magic a hundredfold, but in ordinary circumstances, my aunt was a far more accomplished witch than I was. Yet when Tansy sniffed at the back of the tent, she managed to poke her little head through a gap at the side. "Hey... I think I can get in."

"Hang on a moment." But Tansy had already wriggled through the gap and disappeared. "Tansy?"

A faint squeak of alarm sounded. Heart sinking, I dropped to a crouch and peered under the tent, but it was too dark to see any signs of my familiar. *Oh no.*

"Tansy." I stuck my hand through the opening, but short of ripping the tent open, I had no way inside except through the front.

At the sound of footsteps from around the side of the tent, I stiffened and then rose to my feet.

"I thought I smelled a rat." Aunt Shannon herself came

into view, a squirming Tansy dangling by her tail from her hand. "Missing something?"

"Put her down." So much for my unseen charm. That spell only held up as long as nobody looked too closely at me, and Aunt Shannon had evidently been on the lookout for any trouble outside her tent.

"She was trespassing." She let go of Tansy's tail, and my familiar leapt straight onto my shoulder and wrapped herself around the back of my neck. "Do you think the rules don't apply to you?"

"Speak for yourself." I gestured to her tent. "Did you hear your daughter has been arrested?"

"She most certainly hasn't."

"Rowan, not Vanessa."

She wrinkled her nose. "Are you expecting me to come to her rescue?"

"No." It was a wonder she'd acknowledged her other daughter existed at all. "Just wondered if you heard." She was a good actress, I knew, but there was little point in her pretending that she was ignorant.

"I've been busy," she said. "Unlike your mother, I don't have a personal servant to do all the work for me."

"That's your choice. You could easily afford one."

"I prefer to grow my flowers myself," she said. "It's more satisfying to take credit for my own accomplishments than someone else's."

"Mum does all the work on her flowers herself," I corrected. "Piper isn't a servant."

I was pretty sure Aunt Shannon had had Vanessa performing the exact same tasks as Mum assigned to Piper without paying her for it, though Vanessa seemed content to act as her lapdog. Besides, Piper's main job was to make sure

Aunt Shannon didn't decide to sabotage her flowers or send her familiar to do the same.

Aunt Shannon gave a disdainful sniff. "I'm sure *she* thinks so. See to it that your familiar doesn't put her paws out of bounds again, or next time, I won't be so generous."

Wait, that was it? I'd expected a far harsher warning, but she hadn't even threatened to tell tales on me to my mother. She must be busy—but not, it seemed, with her flower-contest entry. Curiosity urged me to ask Tansy what she'd seen inside the tent, but this might be my last chance to talk to my aunt face to face before the contest. And I really did want to know if she'd had a hand in framing her daughter.

"I will—provided *your* familiar doesn't show up in Rowan's flat while she's gone," I said. "Strangely enough, the substance they found inside her flat as supposed proof of her guilt was a toxin that's deadly to plants. Funny that, don't you think?"

"Not at all."

Her indifferent tone didn't quite convince me, and tension arose in the air. "There's no reason for Rowan to have had her hands on that stuff, but it would certainly come in handy for any entrant in the flower contest. If you know anything about how it might have ended up in Rowan's flat, I'm sure the police would appreciate it if you came forward."

"I have no information to give." Her mouth thinned. "Didn't your mother tell you that involving yourself in a police investigation is not your responsibility?"

"Overseeing the flower contest *is* my responsibility," I said. "I'd say the case is relevant to everyone who plans to enter the contest."

"Then I wish your mother the best of luck tomorrow." She vanished into her tent without another word.

I was tempted to call her back and demand to know what she was playing at. If not her, who had planted the so-called evidence in Rowan's room? Who would *want* to?

"Weird," Tansy said in my ear. "You know what was in that tent? A load of boxes. She still hasn't actually done anything with them."

"Seriously?" This situation just got more and more perplexing. "I didn't expect a confession, but I hoped for *one* answer instead of more questions. I know she's been here during most of the window in which she might have put the evidence in Rowan's flat..."

"That doesn't mean she didn't put it there," said Tansy. "It might even have been hidden there since Saturday."

"If so, it's lucky Rowan didn't find it herself before the police did," I remarked. "Or unlucky, rather."

My aunt was perfectly capable of playing a long game. She'd proven as much already... and I should have known better than to think she'd leave my cousin in peace.

Tansy's tail wrapped around my neck from behind, a comforting gesture. "She won't get away with this, one way or another."

As I'd predicted, my mother woke me at the crack of dawn, requesting my help in setting up the flower contest before the rest of the entrants showed up. I'd barely slept due to worrying about Rowan and the potential consequences for everyone if the contest went sideways, but I didn't even have time to grab a coffee before she ushered me out of the house.

At least I wasn't alone. Piper had to suffer alongside me as the person in charge of transporting Mum's roses to the carnival field without so much as a petal ending up out of place. She'd strapped them to a cart that trundled along the path through the woods at her command, which Mum kept in the shed all year round for such occasions.

Pity the momentousness of the contest didn't erase the fact that my cousin was currently in jail, unable to plead her innocence because the majority of the town's small police force was assigned to guard the carnival instead. Not that anyone would appreciate me pointing that out.

Mum insisted on circling the carnival to check on the defences before leading me to the flower tent. There, we met Leanne, the head judge, a rail-thin witch with wispy grey hair and a frayed black hat decorated with posies that she wore every year. Like the flower club, she'd been a fixation here in Wildwood Heath since before I was born. I had to wonder if she personally knew any of the club members herself, but Mum trusted Leanne and her fellow judges enough not to be biased, and I had quite enough suspects on my list already.

"Robin is going to be casting detection spells on all the contenders and their offerings," Mum told Leanne. "I believe it's prudent given the circumstances."

"Yes, I quite agree," said the elderly witch, peering at me. "Head Witch, it is an honour to finally meet you."

"Uh—good to meet you too." I was far from in the right frame of mind to put on my Head Witch hat, much less make small talk, but Mum wasn't content to let me stand idle and wait for the contest to start. She had both Leanne and me run around and cast detection charms on the tent to make sure nobody had booby-trapped the place overnight before Piper wheeled the cart into the tent and set up Mum's roses upon the table she'd chosen.

The other tables were bare for now, though the stage at

the front of the tent reminded me that I'd forgotten to find the town's mayor and ask what arrangement he'd made with Aunt Shannon. It didn't particularly matter at this point, but evidently, Mum had lost that argument. I hoped she'd been able to take credit for the stage herself, at the very least.

When the other contenders began to arrive, dressed in their finest and laden with bright flowers, my heart gave a nervous flip at the prospect of using my sceptre on all of them. At least a detection spell was fairly straightforward and easy to remember, but I could just imagine how Aunt Shannon would react to me pointing my deadly magical weapon into her face.

"Where's your sister?" I whispered to Mum, noticing one obvious absence from the tent.

"I'd like to know that myself." She watched the tent opening like a hawk until Aunt Shannon finally showed up with Vanessa in tow, a cart of flowers trundling behind her. By this point, everyone else had already set up their displays on the tables that lined every wall of the tent except for the stage at the front.

Aunt Shannon didn't apologise for her lateness, though she did stop to speak to the judges while Vanessa arranged her flowers. Vanessa didn't seem to mind being ordered around, and I was willing to bet Aunt Shannon had entirely handed the responsibility for her flowers to her eldest daughter while she worked on her own schemes.

Did they involve thorn-killer toxin, though? That I didn't know. Yet.

I didn't hear what my aunt said to the judges despite straining my ears, but a moment later, they all climbed onto the stage. Aside from Leanne, I didn't know any of their names, but they weren't flower club members. A few were present—I recognised Araminta's bottle-blond hair on the opposite side of the tent—but I hadn't seen the daisy-haired witch yet.

With the crackle of an amplifying spell, Mum called everyone to attention from the stage.

"Welcome," she said. "I'm delighted to present our annual flower contest, and I will do my best to make this as fulfilling for you as my mother did."

Murmurs filled the tent, and several of the witches' gazes went towards me, as if to question why I wasn't the one making the announcements. The job usually went to the coven leader and not the Head Witch, even when the coven leader was participating in the contest herself, but their whispers made me twitchy, especially when I spotted the smirk on Araminta's face as one of her fellow flower club witches whispered in her ear. *Where is that daisy-haired witch, though?*

"I trust that everyone is on their best behaviour," Mum went on. "But before the contest can begin, I would like to request that each of you leave your wand in the box by the door if you haven't already. When you've done so, return to your tables, and the Head Witch will use a detection charm on each of you."

More whispers followed but no loud objections. As we'd planned, I crossed to the front of the tent as everyone else returned to their tables, including my mother. I started with her, and while Mum's face was expressionless when I lifted the sceptre and cast the detection charm, Piper gave me an encouraging nod. I then moved around the circle of tables, finding myself glad of my lessons with Grandma the previous day. The practise had eased my nerves somewhat, which came in handy when it was Aunt Shannon's turn and I found myself facing the mirrored glares of her and her eldest daughter.

"I can't believe she has *you* checking everyone for cheating," Vanessa hissed. "I suppose that doesn't count as favouritism in her eyes, does it?"

"A detection charm is as impartial as you can get." I raised the sceptre, and they both moved imperceptibly as if anticipating an attack.

I waved the sceptre, part of me expecting a web of green light to appear to indicate foul play, but nothing did. They were squeaky clean, at least on the surface, but what had I expected? A neon sign pointing to their guilt?

I did my level best to ignore Aunt Shannon's satisfied smirk as I moved on to the next entrant. When I reached the end, my arms were aching, and I had a headache brewing. More perplexingly, I hadn't seen any signs of the daisy-haired witch whatsoever.

Since I wasn't a judge or an entrant, I had no reason to stick around, especially as nobody was openly bending the rules, so I went to rescue Piper.

"Find anything?" she whispered when I returned to Mum's table.

"Nope," I said. "Not that I thought there'd be anything out in the open, especially now."

"Nah, if they cheated, they'll have hidden the evidence before the contest started."

Yeah. Or put the evidence in Rowan's flat. "I don't expect this to be the end of it. I'm going to have a look for Tansy outside. Want to come?"

Tansy had been banished from the tent, along with most other familiars, so they wouldn't chew on the flowers. Since Tansy had a liking for sunflower seeds, that was probably a good idea, but I hoped she hadn't got herself into trouble again. Admittedly, my aunt wasn't actually *in* her tent at the moment, but that didn't mean she'd left it unguarded.

"Nah, one of us ought to keep an eye out for any funny business," Piper said. "I'll tell your mum where you are if she comes asking."

I ducked out of the tent, hoping my mother wouldn't raise a fuss at me for leaving the contest. I'd be back before the results were announced, and if anything happened, it was more likely to be on the outside of the tent than on the inside.

"You're hard to get hold of." A familiar voice greeted me on the other side of the tent. I looked up, startled to see Harvey standing there, looking as if he'd just stepped off a broomstick. He wore the lightweight clothes he usually did when flying, and his dark hair was considerably windswept.

"Harvey?" I blinked at him. "What are you doing here?"

"I figured I'd drop by on my way to practise," he said. "Is the contest over already?"

"Nah, it's in progress," I said. "I was in charge of checking for potential cheating, but I couldn't find any, and if I have to stare at one more flower, my eyeballs will melt."

"Best avoid that." He wrapped me in a hug. "Sorry about your cousin. I wish I could do something to help."

"This helps." I hugged him back. "Sorry I haven't been in touch all week."

"I really don't blame you for that, Robin." He kissed me, and I leaned into his embrace.

Someone cleared his throat nearby. I pulled back to see Ramsey standing behind Harvey, wearing his most disapproving expression. "Robin, a word, please."

10

———

R amsey stared pointedly at me until I let go of Harvey. I didn't get what the deal was, given that he'd agreed to stay out of my romantic life, though he probably drew the line at public affection.

"Yes?" I raised a brow at my brother. "What is it?"

"Aren't you supposed to be in there?" He indicated the flower tent.

"I've already done my part," I told him. "Nobody in the contest smuggled in anything illegal, and their wands are currently in a box. Anyway, as I was just saying to Harvey—"

"It didn't look like you were saying anything to me."

"Ha." What was he even doing here? "Don't you have a suspect to question?"

Harvey shifted uncomfortably on his feet. "I should go. My practise session starts soon—I just thought I'd drop by and see how things were going."

"They're going fine," Ramsey said without looking at him. "I'd like to talk to my sister."

Harvey gave me an apologetic look and a wave before walking away under my brother's watchful eye.

"Thanks a bunch," I said to Ramsey. "You don't even know things are going fine, since you just got here."

"Neither do you, since you're out here and not in there."

Someone was in a mood today. "Don't you trust Mum to keep things under control? Besides, I came to find Tansy. All familiars were banished from the tent... including a certain magpie."

I glanced towards Aunt Shannon's tent, but I knew telling my brother about Tansy's attempt to get inside the previous day would not help my cause.

"Myrtle isn't near the café. I checked."

"You're still watching the place?" I asked. "Even though Rowan isn't there?"

The faintest flush lit his cheeks. "Yes. I didn't want things to turn out like this, you know."

"Rowan is okay, though?" Guilt surged inside me for not asking sooner. "Even after spending the night in jail?"

"She's not in the jail, just the holding cells."

"It's not exactly a five-star hotel," I said. "I take it you haven't had time to arrange her trial yet?"

I had little energy to spare for an argument with my brother, but helping at a flower contest instead of the investigation grated on my nerves like sandpaper, and it would be far worse for Rowan.

"I will," he said. "If contradictory information comes to light, she'll be freed sooner."

"You mean about who originally had the thorn-killer toxin?" I queried. "Nobody here brought anything at all. I did check, but it's more likely to have been used *before* the contest."

"That's true," said Ramsey. "There's your familiar."

Tansy came scampering along towards me and halted at my feet. "Hey, Ramsey. Here to arrest someone?"

"No, I came to see how things were getting on," he said. "Robin hasn't found any traces of cheating."

"Did you expect me to?" I asked. "Listen—if the thorn-killer toxin was used on any contest entrants, is it possible to get a list of anyone who didn't enter or who pulled out at the last minute?"

"I'm sure our mother has that information."

I had my doubts she'd be free to talk to me anytime soon since the contest took precedence, but there must be another way to find out. "Chloe might know, but she's back at the office dealing with paperwork."

Could I get away with a quick excursion to the office to speak to her? Debatable, but the judging process would go on for a while yet, and when Chloe was deeply immersed in work, she often didn't hear the phone ringing. Besides, if anyone had been forced to drop out of the contest at the last minute, I wanted to see for myself if the thorn-killer toxin had been the culprit.

"I can fetch her," Tansy offered.

"Nah, I'll go myself. Can you keep an eye out for trouble while I'm gone?"

Ramsey narrowed his eyes at me. "You'd better be prepared to face the consequences if our mother finds out."

"It'll be worth it if I catch the person who ought to be in Rowan's place." The trouble was that there were too many possible culprits, including Aunt Shannon, and most of them were inside that very tent. "Oh—let me know if you see a witch with daisies in her hair. She doesn't seem to have shown up."

Interesting, given her boasting at the café. If she'd intended to cheat her way to victory, you'd have thought she'd show up in person, right? Unless she was lying low because she'd heard about the shifter's murder.

Ramsey appeared unconcerned by my theory, so I left him behind and walked at a fast stride down the woodland path until I reached the road leading to the witches' headquarters. The building was quieter than usual with most people at the carnival, but when I entered my office, Chloe sat in her usual spot as if it was an ordinary day.

She lifted her head. "Robin—wait, did something happen?"

"Nothing happened," I reassured her. "I had a spare moment, and I wanted to look into something. Do you have a list of the contest entrants?"

She gave me an odd look. "Aside from the one on your desk?"

"Oh." I walked over to the desk and began sifting through papers until I found the right one. "I didn't detect anyone trying to smuggle anything illegal into the contest, but if they used a plant-killing toxin, it would have been before the contest started. Do you know if Mum has a list of entrants who dropped out? Especially ones who might have ranked highly in previous contests?"

"I don't know about a list, but I can find the past records."

Chloe got to her feet and approached the cabinets at the back of the office while I scanned the list of entrants. I couldn't put names to faces with most of them, which was a major drawback, but one of them must be our mysteriously absent daisy-haired witch.

Grandma popped out of a cabinet, startling Chloe. "What are you doing here, Robin? Aren't you supposed to be judging the flower contest?"

"I'm not a judge," I told her. "My job was to detect any sabotage, but there wasn't any... unless it took place before the contest. That's why I'm here."

Chloe surveyed the cabinets. "I could have sworn the records were in here somewhere."

I gave my grandmother's ghost an accusing look. "Have you been moving things around again?"

"Certainly not." She huffed. "Why would you accuse me of such a thing?"

She might well be telling the truth this time, given the disorganised mass of cabinets at the back of the office, but searching all of them would take too long.

"Never mind the past records," I said. "You can find a list of the current flower club members, can't you?"

Chloe brightened, moving to her desk. "That I can do. Hang on."

She tapped a few keys on her laptop while Grandma hovered nearby, looking irritated that nobody was paying her any attention. Seconds later, the printer turned on, and a piece of paper flew out.

I reached out and caught the paper in my hand before returning to my desk and picking up the list of contest entrants. When I compared the two and crossed names off the list, I found only three members who hadn't entered the contest.

"It shouldn't take too much digging to find out if they've met with any unfortunate sabotage," I said. "We could even pay house calls."

"What are you doing?" Grandma demanded. "Those are the members of the flower club."

"That's right," I said. "What was your relationship to them, anyway? Were you ever a member?"

"Certainly not. I was far too busy."

Not too busy to enter the actual flower contest, though. "But you were friends with them. Their leader, Araminta..."

"Yes, yes, we were good friends. What of it?"

"Someone in the flower club initially had the thorn-killer toxin," I explained. "Has that ever been an issue in past contests?"

"Certainly not." She made a noise of outrage. "The flower club members might have got a little competitive, but they didn't mind losing to me."

"They don't seem to be fans of the coven these days," I said. "I heard them talking in the café, and one witch claimed to have got her hands on some thorn-killer toxin— from someone in the coven, in fact."

"Who?" she demanded. "Who said they had thorn-killer toxin?"

"I don't know her name," I said. "She had curly grey hair with daisies braided in... and she's not at the contest today."

"Crystal."

I checked the list and confirmed she was one of the absentee members. "Yes, and I find it interesting that she didn't show up to the contest after all."

"I don't like the way you're speculating about my friends," Grandma said sourly. "I won't listen to another word of this."

"Grandma—" But she'd vanished. "Great."

At least she'd confirmed Crystal's name before she'd gone off in a huff, but I could have used the input of someone who knew all the witches of the flower club and the contest entrants.

"I can find their addresses," Chloe offered. "You should get back to the carnival."

My shoulders slumped. "All right."

Mum might have noticed my absence by now, but I didn't regret leaving. I fully intended to hand over the missing members' names and addresses to Ramsey until he identified the one who'd framed Rowan.

I left the office and retraced my steps along the woodland path to the carnival. The volume of noise from that direction had begun to increase, but it seemed more everyday noise than a sign of trouble. The flower tent had opened its doors to the public as the contest advanced so everyone could admire the entrants' displays before the winner was chosen.

I found my brother standing stiffly outside the tent... and then spotted our dad hovering awkwardly at his side. *Oh no.*

"Dad." What was he doing here? Had he been talking to Ramsey? Evidently not, judging from the way the two weren't making eye contact with one another.

"Robin." Dad smiled at me. "Your brother said you were on your way back."

"Ah. Yeah... I dropped back at the office to talk to Chloe." I glanced at Ramsey, who hadn't moved an inch and who acted as if he was made out of stone. "I guess you heard about Rowan?"

"I did," Dad said. "I wanted to come and offer moral support if you needed it."

"I appreciate it." My brother's silently judging presence somewhat overshadowed my words, so I swivelled towards him. "No trouble here?"

"No, and you're very lucky our mother hasn't noticed your absence yet," Ramsey said, still not looking at Dad. "Was it worth it?"

"Might be." I ignored the sarcastic tint to his words. "I have a list of three contest entrants who dropped out at the last minute—and one of them was the witch I overheard in the café."

"The one who was bragging about having that thorn-killer toxin stuff?" Dad faltered when Ramsey's eyes narrowed, though he targeted his glare at me.

"Do *not* talk about that in the open, Robin."

I raised my hands. "Hey, she was the one openly bragging in public. I'm surprised none of the other customers were paying attention."

Or maybe they had been, and someone else in the café had swiped the thorn-killer toxin from her while she'd been busy talking herself up. It wasn't the least plausible theory.

Ramsey's jaw clenched, and while he refrained from sparing so much as a glance for Dad, he seemed to have forgotten that our father had been a witness too. I felt a rush of annoyance towards my brother for making things unnecessarily difficult. Maybe I should have tried harder to make the two reconcile with one another from the start, but I'd been fighting a losing battle, and I'd never expected Rowan's freedom might depend upon their willingness to talk to one another.

Before I could say another word, Ramsey had walked away, disappearing around the side of the tent.

I shook my head as I looked after him. "Honestly. I'm sorry, Dad."

"It's fine," he said. "Part of me expected it to go worse than it did."

"You must have had low expectations." At least Mum hadn't emerged from the tent and thrown herself into the fray as well, kicking off a family conflict straight from the days when the four of us had lived under the same roof. I suppressed a shudder at the thought. Some things were better off left in the past.

"I shouldn't have come here, I know," he went on. "I wish there was more I could do for your cousin, though. I can't believe Ramsey actually arrested her."

"Someone planted the so-called evidence directly in her flat," I said. "I have Chloe looking into any possible dropouts from the contest who might have had their beloved plants tampered with, but Ramsey doesn't seem in a hurry to look into it."

"I hope you can convince him," said Dad. "Might be easier when I'm not here."

I gave him a hug. "Some of us appreciate you being here."

I knew that wouldn't erase the sting of Ramsey's rejection, but I had to make it clear that the problem was on my brother's end, not his.

After Dad ambled away, I went looking for Ramsey and found him standing on the other side of the flower tent. He hadn't even tried to pretend he'd been doing anything other than avoiding Dad.

Right. I marched over and shoved the paper into his face. "As I was saying before you so rudely turned your back on me, I have a list of the flower club members who dropped out of the contest at the last minute. There are only three, so it's not a stretch to say at least one of them might have had an unexpected incident involving some thorn-killer toxin."

"Yes, it is." His gaze skimmed over the paper. "I don't know those people. Shouldn't you have the coven members memorised by now?"

"They aren't coven members; they're retired." Yes, it would probably help if I'd taken note of everyone's names, but I was still struggling with the endless list of names and titles the Head Witch was supposed to remember, and members of random flower clubs weren't exactly ranked high on my priority list.

"Crystal is our wayward daisy-haired witch—the one I

saw publicly bragging," I added, but he brushed the paper aside. "I'm trying to help."

"The contest results will be announced soon," he said. "I'd advise you to be present when they are."

I peered back into the tent and saw that the judges had gathered in a huddle near the stage. *You haven't won this one yet, Ramsey.* "I'll be right back."

I slipped into the tent and had to navigate around members of the public to reach the table nearest to the stage. It was impossible to disguise my sceptre, and after the third exclamation of "Head Witch!" my mother briefly glanced in my direction, but she didn't otherwise give any indication that she had an opinion on my brief absence.

I made my way to Piper's side, and she whispered, "I told her you were at the office, but she didn't seem impressed. Just a heads-up."

"Figures," I muttered back. "Uh—I don't suppose you're familiar with all the members of the flower club?"

"Nope, because they rejected my membership application." She snorted. "They said I didn't meet the requirements."

"What's that supposed to mean?" I held out the list for her to take. "Meaning you're not retired?"

"Pretty much." She eyed the list. "What's this?"

"The names of the members who dropped out of the contest at the last minute," I whispered. "I wonder if any dropped out because their plants mysteriously died."

"Fair point," she said. "Hmm. Crystal has flu, apparently. Not sure about the other two."

"Crystal is the one I saw in the coffee shop," I said in an undertone. "She has flu? Really?"

"That's what your mother told me," she said. "Why?"

"She was the one bragging about her thorn-killer toxin." *What's she playing at?* "And the others?"

"I have no idea," she said. "You'll have to ask Araminta."

Would she tell me? Debatable, but at that moment, a hush fell over the room as the judges climbed back onto the stage, ready to announce the results of the contest. My heart skipped a beat, and despite my lack of investment in the results, I felt a flutter of apprehension in my chest.

All the entrants had returned to the tables while the members of the public gathered in the large space in the middle of the tent. I spotted Ramsey near the back, though he didn't catch my eye.

I scanned the contest entrants instead. Aunt Shannon and Vanessa both looked almost bored, but when I caught sight of the leader of the flower club, Araminta's expression was intently focused on the stage.

Leanne spoke. "The contest is over, and firstly, we'd like to offer congratulations to our entrants. The standard this year was incredibly high."

A smattering of applause broke out, and then the judge took a deep breath, ready to announce the winner. *Here we go.*

11

"Roxanne Wildwood is the winner of this year's flower contest."

The judge's words echoed in the air for a moment as all eyes turned to Mum. A round of applause arose from the crowd, while my shoulders slumped with relief. At least one thing had gone according to plan, though it didn't surprise me when Leanne's next announcement came.

"The second prize goes to Shannon Wildwood."

As expected, though Aunt Shannon's expression showed mostly indifference as she sailed to the stage to claim her trophy.

"And the third prize will go to Araminta Greenbriar."

The blond leader of the flower club clambered onto the stage and exchanged words with Mum and Aunt Shannon as she took her trophy. Though I didn't hear what she said, the other two both looked mildly annoyed.

Piper exhaled a sigh of relief. "I didn't expect otherwise, but that's a weight off my shoulders."

"Same," I muttered back. "Now we need to find out what happened to the ones who didn't show up."

Leaving the tent again wasn't an option, however, not with Mum standing directly in front of me with her golden trophy in her hands. More applause showered the three winners, and as they left the stage, people flooded in to congratulate them. Mum accepted the praise with grace, though I detected a current of annoyance under the surface, and it didn't entirely surprise me when she cornered me behind her flower display at the first possible opportunity.

"Where have you been?" she demanded. "I thought I told you to watch the contenders."

"I thought I was supposed to cast the detection charms, nothing more." Her anger disarmed me; I'd expected her to be pleased to have won at the very least. "And—er, congratulations?"

"Mother." Ramsey came marching over to us. "I'm glad the contest worked out the way it should have."

"I don't need to hear meaningless praise from my own children," she said. "Robin, you're here as Head Witch."

"Then as Head Witch, please allow me to give you my sincere congratulations." I regretted my impulsive words when she levelled me with a glare. "No, really, I'm glad you won. I wouldn't have left if it hadn't been important."

"What, pray tell, was urgent enough for you to disappear at a crucial time such as this?"

I looked for Piper and spotted her talking to Araminta. Was she asking her about the missing members of her club or just congratulating her? From this angle, I couldn't see the flower club leader's expression, but Mum barred my line of sight, expectantly eyeing me.

"I figured that if nobody smuggled anything illegal into

the contest, they must have cheated beforehand," I said in a low voice. "I went to find out which members of the flower club dropped out at the last minute, and Piper told me that the witch I heard bragging in the coffee shop seems to have come down with flu. The timing seems suspect to me."

"Piper?" She caught sight of Piper and Araminta, and her eyes narrowed. "Did you want her to be distracted from her duties?"

"She volunteered to help me, Mum."

To my utter mortification, my mother strode out from behind the cart and approached Araminta and Piper. Ramsey had vanished into the crowd, while I caught sight of Aunt Shannon nearby with her second-place trophy in her hand. Our gazes briefly connected, and I detected a distinct hint of satisfaction in her eyes. She knew Mum was angry at me.

"Araminta," said Mum. "Sorry, I need to borrow Piper for a second."

I opened my mouth to protest, but Araminta spoke first. "Of course, feel free. It's a pleasure to see the Wildwood Coven's new leader is actively involved in the flower contest, even if the Head Witch isn't."

If that wasn't a jab at me, I was a leprechaun. While Mum dragged Piper away, I flagged down Araminta before Mum could stop me.

"Excuse me," I said.

"Can I help you... Head Witch?" The pause before the last two words was deliberate, I was sure, but I took no notice.

"I hope you can," I said. "I heard about Crystal catching the flu, and I wanted to pass on my commiserations to her at not being able to enter the contest."

Her expression reflected flat blankness. "I'll pass on the kind words to her. I'm sure she'll appreciate your concern."

Her words dripped with insincerity, and that prompted me to add, "And I'm sorry for the others who dropped out too."

"Robin." Mum's voice speared me from behind. "I'd appreciate it if you came with me too."

Steeling myself, I followed her and Piper to the table displaying her roses, on which she'd placed her winning trophy. "I think Araminta isn't being fully truthful," I said.

"I thought not too..." Piper wilted under Mum's glare. "Um. I just meant she didn't seem that disappointed to hear about Ami or Leah dropping out."

"Or Crystal mysteriously catching the flu," I added. "Did she tell you what happened to the other two?"

"No, she was pretty cagey," Piper said, eyeing Mum warily. "I'm surprised Ami didn't enter, to tell you the truth. She's usually a regular."

"That's enough," said Mum. "Robin, was I not clear when I told you to keep your attention on the contest?"

It wouldn't be an issue if I was allowed to leave. "Let me tell Ramsey, at least. It's important to his investigation."

"Fine." Her lips barely moved when she spoke. "This is your last warning to be more careful."

Feeling bad for leaving Piper in the crossfire, I crossed the tent to find my brother standing near the entrance, his monochrome suit forming a stark contrast to the brightness around him. I didn't think he'd appreciate it if I grabbed a stray flower to put in his hair, so I refrained.

"Ramsey, Piper has the names of the other missing flower club members, at least one of whom had no good reason to drop out," I told him. "Can we talk in private?"

"You aren't going to let this one drop, are you?"

"Nope." When a muscle twitched in his jaw, I added, "You know as well as I do that there isn't any thorn-killer toxin here in this tent, but the mysterious absence of the one person who bragged about having some has to be worth a second look. Even if they had innocent reasons for bowing out, it's better to be certain."

He exhaled a sigh. "You're sure the witch you heard in the café is the one who's been stricken down with flu?"

"More like she's hiding," I said. "If she *did* have that thorn-killer toxin in her bag in the café, and someone stole it..."

"You're leaping to a lot of conclusions there, Robin."

"She seemed confident that she'd win. Why else would she go into hiding?" I tensed when someone caught my arm from behind, but it was only Piper.

"Robin—she's there," she whispered. "That's Ami—the other witch who dropped out."

I rotated on my heel, following her line of sight to an unfamiliar curvy witch with short grey hair near the tent's opening. "That's her?"

"Doesn't look like she's here for the contest," Piper muttered. "I can ask why she dropped out."

"I'll ask her." Ignoring Ramsey's exasperated sigh, I crossed the short distance to Ami, who peered at me in surprise.

"Head Witch," she said. "To what do I owe the pleasure?"

"This is an odd question, but I wondered if you had any particular reason for not entering the contest this year. Piper told me you're a regular entrant."

"Yes," she said. "Yes, there was an incident that prevented me from entering. My plants... well, they died. Overnight. All of them."

"Really?" My brows lifted. "Did you know how that might have come about?"

"No, it had me stumped," she said. "It's not the end of the world. I know your mother always wins the contest, but I hoped to have one chance before I retire."

"You don't think it might have been sabotage, do you?" When her eyes rounded, I lowered my voice even further. "If someone else in the club was responsible, would Araminta take it seriously?"

"Undoubtedly," she said. "But it was just an unfortunate accident."

"Were you... were you at the café on Saturday?" I threw caution to the winds. "At Were's My Coffee?"

"No, I wasn't." Her frown deepened. "Any reason?"

"I heard..." I hesitated, trying to figure out how to sound less like I'd been eavesdropping on her fellow flower club members. "There was talk of someone having got their hands on thorn-killer toxin. On the same day, someone else was poisoned to death with the same substance, so we're— the police are looking into any possible connections to the flower contest."

"Poison?" she said. "Someone died?"

How had she not heard? Well, if she'd been busy trying to revive her flowers and hadn't attended the meeting, she might have missed the news. It was obvious that the flower club's members in general didn't have much interaction with the outside world.

"Yes," I said. "Thorn-killer toxin is a rare substance, so it's possible whoever sabotaged your contest entry was also connected to the murder, if indirectly."

She shook her head firmly. "No... nobody has been near my plants in the past week except for me."

"Nobody at all?" I asked. "Have you had any visitors?"

"Why—Araminta dropped by to ask why I wouldn't be attending Saturday's meeting, and I explained that it's hard to get around with my hip the way it is. I shouldn't have walked all the way out here, but I did very much want to look at all the contest entrants." She eyed the tent fondly.

Araminta visited? Interesting. Next to me, Piper shifted on her feet. "Where are your plants now?"

"Oh, they're in my back garden. Why?"

Piper made a coughing noise. "Erm... thorn-killer toxin is highly dangerous to any other plants it comes into contact with."

"What are you doing?" Araminta swept into view. "Are you bothering poor Ami, Head Witch?"

Bothering? She had some nerve stepping in, especially if she was the person who'd sabotaged Ami's plants to begin with. I put on a false smile. "Ami was telling me that her flowers met with an unfortunate accident and she had to drop out of the contest."

"Yes, it's very tragic," Araminta agreed. "There's always next year."

Was it her? I couldn't tell, and if Ami had trouble getting around, then it was entirely possible that someone else had broken into her property and used the thorn-killer toxin on her plants while she hadn't been watching. Someone like Crystal, for instance. Whatever the case, Araminta definitely radiated more condescension than one might expect of someone comforting a friend.

"What day did it happen?" I asked Ami, ignoring the flower club leader's presence.

"Uh... Friday, I think."

"Head Witch," Araminta said in sharp tones. "Didn't I tell you to cease bothering Ami? She's been through quite enough already."

Yes. She has. I hitched my false smile back into place. "Yes, it's an awful shame. It's very lucky that the same didn't happen to you, isn't it?"

I turned away, beckoning Piper to come with me, and we left both witches behind. I tracked down an irate Ramsey, whose manner suggested he'd overheard our entire exchange. "Robin, you must stop this ridiculousness. Araminta is a former coven member, and—"

"Ami's plants mysteriously died, and Araminta was the last person to pay her a visit, Ramsey," I cut in. "Piper, would you be able to tell if someone used thorn-killer toxin on Ami's plants?"

"Yes," she said. "I'd need to see them for myself, but yes, absolutely."

She'd need to ask Mum's permission to leave, which was another issue entirely, but I'd had about enough of my brother looking at me as if I'd done a striptease on the stage in front of the elderly witches. "Ramsey, there's no need for that look. Frankly, I think Ami was grateful for us rescuing her from Araminta."

"You can't throw around baseless accusations, Robin," he said. "Not without consequences."

"I won't shed a tear if I'm banned from the flower club." I saw the alarm on Piper's face and turned around to see Mum had come out of the tent in time to overhear us.

"Robin, what *are* you playing at this time?" she said.

"Ami's plants were sabotaged," I told her. "The only way to be certain that thorn-killer toxin was responsible is for an expert to look. You can spare Piper for an hour, can't you?"

"Now is not the time."

"Then when?" The words slipped out through gritted teeth. "My cousin is sitting in a jail cell for a murder she didn't commit. She might even end up losing her job and home over this. Does that not matter to you at all?"

"Have you not an ounce of decorum in you?" Her expression stilled, and I spotted Aunt Shannon approaching us with impeccable timing as usual.

"Hello, Head Witch," she said. "I seem to have interrupted at a bad time."

The smirk on Aunt Shannon's face made it clear that she was aware she'd walked straight into an argument between Mum and me, but I wasn't about to rise to her bait.

"It's no concern of yours," I said in my falsest polite tones. "My mother and I were discussing the ongoing murder investigation."

"Ah, yes, my daughter's unfortunate situation must be quite distressing for you," said Aunt Shannon. "I hope Rowan's given a fair trial, at the least."

"She won't need one when we find out who planted that thorn-killer toxin in her room," I told her. "Since she has no reason to have obtained it herself and has no link to the murder victim, I've no doubt she'll be out of there in no time."

"I'm glad you think so." Her demure smile gave nothing away, but whether she was genuinely involved herself or had simply taken the opportunity to taunt me didn't matter at this point. I needed to find out if the thorn-killer toxin had indeed been used against Ami's flowers before I made any accusations.

As Aunt Shannon turned away, Mum strode after her. For once, I didn't much care if they got into a public fight, because at least it meant I was no longer on the receiving end of my mother's wrath.

I swivelled back to my brother. "If those two get into a

duel, both of you will have to take back every word you said about me acting inappropriately."

"Don't be absurd," he said. "Our mother is under a lot of stress, and while I realise that you're concerned for our cousin, there's a time and a place for this discussion, and this isn't it."

"I'm pretty sure the timing is deliberate," I corrected. "Whoever murdered that shifter wanted to strike while the police's attention was on the carnival, and besides, the main part of the contest is over. Mum already won."

Piper sucked in a breath. "Ami's back. I'll see if I can convince your mother to let me go and look at her plants."

Mum sure as hell wouldn't listen to me, so I figured it couldn't hurt. "See what she says."

When she walked off, I was left with my brother, whose body language suggested he had no intention of letting me out of his sight. I had a suspicion that Ramsey knew I was in the right and that he was stubbornly digging his heels in for the sake of it, but that didn't mean he intended to lose the argument. He was too obstinate.

Unfortunately, even if my hunch was right and Ami had been the unlucky victim of the thorn-killer toxin's original owner, it left an awful lot of questions unanswered. Such as how the toxin's owner had obtained the substance and how it had ended up in Rowan's flat after the murder. Finding proof that someone had killed Ami's plants wouldn't get my cousin off the hook, and I was still at a loss to explain how nobody had noticed the break-in. The flower club witches weren't what you would call subtle, and you'd think someone would have noticed if any of them had come back to the café on the day of the murder.

Had Ramsey asked Mal and the other staff members? I didn't know, but anything they might have uncovered while searching the property had been overshadowed by their discovery of the thorn-killer toxin in Rowan's flat.

Ramsey turned back to me. "You're being quiet. That's usually a bad sign."

I feigned a gasp. "I'm going to ignore the insult there and point out that I've been here since the crack of dawn, and I'm falling asleep on my feet."

"Then buy a coffee."

"It's not the same if it isn't from Were's My Coffee?" My jaw cracked in a yawn. "Also, I'm guessing Ami wasn't supposed to actually show up to the contest today. Araminta didn't seem pleased to see her."

"You don't think her displeasure was due to seeing the Head Witch interrogating her fellow witches, then?"

"Partly, but not for the reasons you're probably thinking." I gave him a sideways look. "You saw her attitude for yourself. It's not hard to imagine her poisoning her rivals' flowers, is it?"

"It's my job to look at facts, not imaginary scenarios."

"Then look at Ami's plants." I dropped my voice as Piper led a confused-looking Ami back into view.

"Hey, Ramsey," said Piper. "I'm going to Ami's house to look at her plants, and I think you ought to come with me to verify if there was any sabotage."

"My mother gave you permission?" Ramsey eyed Ami, whose expression showed vague puzzlement. "Do you think there was sabotage?"

"Well... I don't think it's worth the bother, but if the coven leader's personal gardener believes something is amiss, who am I to say no?"

I held my breath, half expecting him to refuse, but my brother inclined his head. "I will come and look. Robin, you stay here."

I made to follow anyway, and my phone buzzed in my pocket. I fished it out and found a message from Chloe listing the addresses of the three flower club members who hadn't been present at the contest.

"I have the other addresses," I told Ramsey. "Including Crystal's. I'd like to know if she really has flu, wouldn't you?"

"I could have found their addresses myself," he said while Ami looked on curiously. "Also, not entering the contest doesn't mean there was any sabotage involved."

"I know." I turned to Piper. "I'll meet you after you've been to Ami's house, okay?"

"Wait, where are you going?" She glanced at my brother, whose jaw tightened in annoyance. "I have permission to go to Ami's house, but you don't, Robin. Sorry."

"Lucky I'm not going there."

"Okay, then." Piper's eyes glittered with amusement. "C'mon, Ami."

Ramsey gave me a last warning look to tell me not to follow them, which I ignored as I went in search of my familiar. It took several minutes for me to track her down behind Aunt Shannon's tent, where she'd dug a sizeable hole. "Whoa, Tansy. What are you doing?"

"Digging a tunnel underneath."

"Watch you don't get stuck in there," I said. "I'm heading off for a bit."

"Where to?"

"The café, to start off with," I decided. "I want another word with Mal, and then I'll see if Crystal really does have flu. I'd say she's more likely to be lying low."

Tansy flicked more mud off her paws. "Want me to come with you?"

"I could use someone to keep an eye out here, since Ramsey and Piper just left too." My brother had also driven my dad away, which I still needed to deal with, but Rowan had been stuck in prison for long enough already.

"Good luck." Tansy returned to her digging, and I hoped she'd be careful to avoid getting herself into trouble while I was gone. Aunt Shannon's attention was still on the flower tent, but it'd be just like her to strike when my back was turned.

If she broke into Rowan's flat, I need to find the proof.

12

———

I didn't know if visiting the café would bring me any answers, but the tantalising smell of coffee beans was too much to resist. There were few customers inside, but the place was still open, so I pushed the door inward and entered. I didn't see Mal, though I recognised the barista at the counter as one of the staff who'd been with Rowan on the day of the murder. The tall and skinny shifter's name badge read *Richie*.

"Head Witch." He paled when he saw me—or, more specifically, the sceptre. "Ah... can I help you?"

"Sure," I said. "I'd like a word with your boss. Is Mal in?"

"He's in the back. I'll get him."

He all but fled into the back room, while the handful of patrons in the café all looked in my direction. Not for the first time, I wished I was allowed to leave my sceptre behind while running errands. Granted, I was still on duty as Head Witch, even if I wasn't acting with the permission of my coven leader, but that didn't mean I wanted to draw unnecessary attention.

I also knew I was pushing my luck by defying my

mother when she was already in a tetchy mood, but there was little I could do at the carnival and a lot I could do out here. If I could find any evidence pointing to the person who'd put that thorn-killer toxin in Rowan's room, it'd be a starting point.

My phone buzzed loudly in my pocket. I checked the number calling—Mum—and turned my phone off to quieten the noise. *Oh boy. She's mad at me.*

A moment later, Mal emerged from the back room, looking surprised to see me. "Head Witch."

"Hey," I said. "Sorry, I just had a question or two."

"About Rowan?"

"Yeah... or whoever could have got upstairs into her flat to plant the evidence in there." I kept my voice low, conscious of the patrons, whose whispers suggested they were curious to know why the Head Witch was in the middle of town and not at the carnival. "My brother is close to finding out who originally had the thorn-killer toxin that was used to poison the victim, but there's still the question of how it got into Rowan's flat."

He cleared his throat. "I see. You know I believe in your cousin's innocence, but I didn't see or hear anyone go to the upper floor on the day of the murder. The only people with access are me and Rowan herself. There's the window..."

"We put a net over the window to keep out any... uh, airborne trespassers," I explained. "Did you see any of the customers return to the café after you closed up?"

"On Saturday, you mean?" he said. "No, but I was cleaning up in the back room. A couple of my staff told me we had a few people drop by to ask why we were closed, but none of the initial customers. Is there anyone in particular you had in mind?"

"The flower club members are regulars here, right?"

"As of a few weeks ago, yes," he said. "I'm not entirely sure who gave them the recommendation that caused them to pick out our café for their informal gatherings, and they can be a little rowdy, but do the police really suspect them of murder?"

"You know I told you the substance used to poison the victim can also be used to kill plants?" I asked. "Turns out someone *did* use it on another contender's plants before the contest today."

His eyes widened. "The contest... is it already over?"

"Yes, and Lady Wildwood—my mother—was the winner."

"Oh, that's great news," he said. "Tell her I said congratulations."

"I will." Annoyance twinged at me for the change of subject, though it was understandable that anyone unable to attend the contest would be interested to know the result. "We're trying to find out if anyone dropped out at the last minute, and there were a few, including the daisy-haired witch I mentioned seeing in here before the murder. Crystal, her name is."

"Doesn't ring a bell," he said. "Have you told your brother? Seems to me that he could make use of this information more than I could."

"Yes, but he wasn't here at the café when I witnessed their conversation," I explained. "It's possible the evidence was planted in Rowan's room right after the murder, when everyone was distracted."

"I see," he said. "I was in the back room until the police showed up, but I'd have heard if anyone had gone up to Rowan's room, since it's directly above."

"Had she left the café since Saturday?" I queried.

"Not to my knowledge." His brow wrinkled. "You visited

her on Saturday night, didn't you? That's the last time I remember anyone coming in. We weren't open on Sunday."

"I know." The drink had definitely been poisoned at some point when we'd all been in the café, but that didn't mean the thorn-killer toxin had been planted in Rowan's flat at that same time. Someone might have sneaked upstairs in the short window before the police had shown up, though there'd also been a couple of hours between the café's early closure and my arrival at Rowan's flat that evening.

Come to think of it, Ramsey's familiar had been watching the café in person since the police had left, which meant either the killer had operated within that one short window—or they'd used magic to sneak in.

"I'll have a think," he added. "See if I can recall anything else."

"Thanks." I made to leave and nearly collided with the barista from earlier, who'd skirted the counter with a tray of drinks in his hands. "Whoa. Sorry."

He backed up a few steps, narrowly avoiding dropping the tray. "Ah—sorry, Head Witch."

I watched him drop the drinks off at the nearest table, my mind ticking over the possibilities. The boss had had all the staff cleaning up after the police had left, so it was possible one of them had seen something their boss hadn't.

After Richie had served the customers their drinks, I waylaid him. "Excuse me. Weird question, but I wondered if you saw anyone come back to the café on Saturday after the police left."

He blinked. "Y—yes. We stayed to clean the place for a couple of hours, and we had to turn away a few customers who didn't realise we were closed."

"You were all cleaning? Including Rowan?"

"Of course."

She'd been downstairs, leaving her flat unattended, and since the door to access her flat was on the outside, it was possible someone had slipped down the side alley and crept in while everyone was cleaning up the aftermath.

"Did you come back on Sunday?" I asked.

"No," he said. "We were all given the day off. I hoped to go to the carnival, but it wasn't open yet."

Now it was, but he'd drawn the short straw in having to work today, evidently.

"Did any of the customers who'd been in the café earlier that day come back?" I asked. "Such as those flower club members? You remember them, right?"

He winced, presumably recalling how rudely they'd treated him. "They didn't come back, but... well, I did see that shifter. The guy who was with the... with the..."

"The victim?"

"Him. Yeah." He looked down. "I don't want to get anyone into trouble, but I saw him outside the café an hour or so after we closed."

"He came back?" I asked. "Why?"

"I don't know."

Had he already known he was going to be questioned by the police the following day? He must have, but his reappearance didn't make much sense. Was it worth mentioning to Ramsey? I didn't particularly want another potentially innocent person to end up in hot water, but if none of the flower club members had been spotted outside the café, I'd have to find proof elsewhere.

I left the café and found Piper waiting outside. "Oh, hey. Have you already been to Ami's house?"

"Yep," she said. "You were right. Her entire garden's a wasteland."

"Thorn-killer toxin?"

"Undoubtedly," she said. "Were you talking to Rowan's boss?"

"And landlord." *For now,* said a voice in the back of my mind that I couldn't quite tamp down. What would happen if Rowan was stuck in a cell for weeks? The café was popular these days, as was proven by the flower club's sudden interest in using it as a base, and if they needed more staff to handle the influx of customers, would Rowan end up being replaced? She needed that job to pay rent on her upstairs flat, and it was hard not to imagine the whole arrangement falling to pieces if I didn't get her out of jail.

"Why'd you come back?" Piper asked. "To look around?"

"I hoped someone would have seen one of the flower club members lurking around after the café had closed on Saturday," I admitted. "I need proof they put the evidence in Rowan's room, but the barista told me he didn't see any of them. Though he did see that shifter—you know, the murder victim's friend."

"Oh." Her brow wrinkled. "It'd be easier if we had a more direct line pointing to the culprit, for sure. Someone definitely poisoned Ami's flowers, but there's nothing to tie that to the incident on Saturday."

"Her plants were poisoned before the murder, right?"

"Yes," she said. "Also, from the way my phone is blowing up, I think we should head back to the carnival before your mother sends out a search party."

"I turned mine off." I grimaced. "Where'd Ramsey go?"

"He wanted to talk to Ami in private and then drop by Crystal's house," she said. "Your mum doesn't seem to be hounding *him,* but she wants me back at the flower tent. I figured I'd warn you."

"She'll have to wait," I said. "That Crystal had the thorn-killer toxin with her in the café. I know it."

"Then why'd she drop out?" she queried.

"At a guess, someone stole the thorn-killer toxin from her before she could use it."

Like Dale Longfoot? I hadn't pegged him as the killer, but he'd been closest to the victim and had also been sitting next to the flower club's table. If he'd swiped the thorn-killer toxin from the witches and then put it in Rowan's room after murdering his friend, he'd have effectively covered all their tracks at the same time. It didn't explain why poor Rowan had been chosen to take the heat, but she did live right above the café, so the shifter's choice might have been practical rather than malicious.

"All right," she said. "Good luck. I'll try to convince your mother to soften the blow."

If I'd had a scrap of self-preservation left, I'd have followed her, but I wanted a word with my brother away from Mum's judgemental presence.

I walked the short distance to the police station and found my dad, of all people, waiting outside.

"Dad." I halted. "Erm... what are you doing here?"

"Looking for you," he said. "I saw you left the carnival and wondered if you were in trouble."

"No more than the usual." I peered through the front doors, but as I'd thought, my brother wasn't yet back from questioning the flower club witches. "I was asking the café's staff if they saw anyone hanging around on Saturday after the murder. I hoped to find out who might have sneaked into Rowan's room to plant the evidence, but the person they saw isn't who I expected, so I'm at a loss."

"Was it Dale?"

"Yes... why?" I asked. "Do you know him?"

"Not well, but like I told you, he's part of the pack, and

when I asked Jessica if she knew him, she mentioned that the two of them—"

"Robin, what did I tell you about sharing information about the investigation with members of the public?" Ramsey walked up to us, his arms crossed over his chest in annoyance. "What are you doing here?"

"Giving you relevant information," I said, having had about enough of his habit of pointedly ignoring our father when he was standing right there. "Dad's here to do the same."

Dad startled. "Robin, I don't think—"

"Like what?" Ramsey finally looked at Dad, though he avoided making eye contact with him. "If you know something pertinent to the investigation, why didn't you come forward sooner?"

"Because... well..." Dad stuttered.

"Ramsey!" I snapped. "Can you take off the suit and tie for one second and talk like an actual human?"

"This is my job, Robin," he retaliated. "Not yours, and not whoever you want to drag into this."

"I came here on my own account," Dad mumbled. "And I didn't—I assumed you spoke to Dale yourself, but from what Robin said, he didn't share everything."

He glared at me then looked back at Dad. "In that case, I'd appreciate it if you shared the information you found out."

"It's not exactly information," he said. "Jessica, my wife —she knew the victim, and she knows Dale too. There... there might be a history between the two that wasn't made clear when you questioned Dale."

Ramsey drew in a breath. "I'll talk to him again if it becomes necessary. Thank you for letting me know."

"I have information too," I added. "One of the baristas at

the café saw Dale outside on Saturday while they were tidying up after the police left."

He blinked. "And this is relevant... why?"

"Because someone planted that thorn-killer toxin in Rowan's flat, and I thought it might be one of the flower club members," I explained. "There's a short time in which they could have got into her flat while she wasn't there, and the staff were downstairs for a couple of hours, helping their boss clean up after the customers left. Was your familiar already there?"

"Not yet, no." Ramsey's gaze flickered towards Dad, his jaw tightening in annoyance.

Dad cleared his throat. "Jessica said she doesn't think Dale's likely to be the murderer, Robin... and why would he frame your cousin if he was?"

I might have voiced my earlier theory about the killer taking advantage of Rowan's position, but the irritation radiating from Ramsey prompted me to say, "Ramsey, stop looking at us like that. Can't you see we're both trying to help you?"

"You're trying to derail me," he corrected. "I thought you wanted me to visit those other two witches who dropped out of the contest."

"Yes—start with Crystal," I said. "She certainly *had* the thorn-killer toxin at one point, as I heard—"

"No, you can't come with me," Ramsey interjected. "You have to go back to the carnival. I appreciate your concern for our cousin, but our mother needs your help."

"The contest is over, Ramsey," I said. "Our mother wouldn't even accept my congratulations on her victory, so I get the impression I'm better off staying out of her hair. Besides, Piper's already gone back."

And I'd left Tansy to keep an eye on Aunt Shannon,

though I hoped my aunt hadn't realised that a very determined squirrel was in the process of digging her way into her tent. *Hmm. Maybe I should find her before she gets caught.* I dearly wanted to see how Crystal tried to justify herself to my brother, but if I went to her house and called her out on her possession of the thorn-killer toxin, I'd have to admit I'd overheard her discussing me behind my back.

"I will tell you *and* our mother every detail of the questioning when I return to the carnival," Ramsey said firmly. "Now, will you leave?"

I thought about asking to see Rowan, but that would be pushing my luck, and it wasn't like I had a solid plan for getting her out of jail. *Yet.* "Fine."

As Dad and I walked back through Wildwood Heath, I'd rarely seen the streets so quiet, though the sounds of the carnival filled the background.

"Sorry," Dad said. "I feel like I made things worse back there, not better."

"Nah, Ramsey's always like that," I said. "I'd follow him to Crystal's house if he'd let me, but that won't end well. I'm sure she's the one behind all this."

"Then we'll trust Ramsey to catch her in the act."

I hoped he was right. Personally, I thought Dad's faith in him was more than my brother deserved after how Ramsey had treated him... though maybe it was Mum I ought to worry about. I hadn't quite got up the nerve to turn my phone back on yet and face all the messages she'd no doubt left for me.

When we reached the field, I halted and turned to Dad. "You might want to stay at a safe distance while I check on Mum."

"Good call." Like me, he'd figured that seeing her ex-husband would not improve Mum's mood.

Bracing myself, I walked into the main tent, where I found myself nose-to-nose with my mother. Her expression could have frozen an entire lake, and I backed straight out of the tent again as she cornered me outside.

"Robin, did I not make myself clear when I told you not to go off alone?" she said, thin-lipped. "I've called Chloe, and she's expecting you back at the office within ten minutes, or else she'll come to get you herself. You're going to stay put until the end of the workday, at which point you'll come back here to witness the evening ceremony at the carnival."

My mouth fell open. She hadn't given me an ultimatum like this in a long time, not since before I'd left home in my late teens. Certainly not after I'd become Head Witch.

"Mum," I said delicately. "I'm sorry I ignored your orders, but we found proof that Ami's plants were sabotaged before the contest, and Ramsey is visiting Crystal right this instant—"

"Then leave it to him," she said. "Risking his safety is in his job description, but yours is at risk every time you leave your home, *especially* with our doors open to the public and most of the police centred around the field. Wandering off alone is all but an invitation to anyone who might wish you harm."

"I wasn't alone," I said, though I already knew I was losing the argument. "There was hardly anyone around."

"And what about everyone in this tent who had to witness the Head Witch disappearing at an inappropriate time?" she said. "I've covered for you for long enough."

"And your sister?" I challenged her. "Why does she get a pass and not me? She's as much under your authority as I am—if not more—but you're more concerned with keeping up appearances than calling her to account."

"That, Robin, is between my sister and me. Not you. Now, leave."

The urge hit me to dig in my heels. But knowing Mum, she probably would force poor Chloe to march me back to the office, and my assistant didn't deserve to deal with the fallout of my own choices.

If Ramsey came back with proof that Crystal had held the thorn-killer toxin in her hands, it might cause Mum to loosen her grip, and I'd get a second chance to explain. We were close to answers. I knew it.

13

_____

Chloe met me at the door to my office, wearing an apologetic expression. "I tried to make her see reason; I really did."

"It's not your fault." I returned to my desk and sank into the chair. "I'm the one who kept pushing her buttons and ignoring the warning signs. If the murderer had picked literally any other weekend to strike, it would have been appreciated. Well, not really, but you know what I mean."

"I do know," she said. "I wonder if they picked the weekend of the carnival precisely because they knew your family would be distracted."

"I thought so—and the police too," I added. "It'd have taken ages for them to show up at the café after the murder if Ramsey hadn't been around. I'm not sure why he wasn't at the carnival, in fact."

Unless he'd been watching Dad and me, but that made zero sense. It did remind me that I'd left poor Dad back in the field without being able to tell him where I'd gone. Not to mention Tansy, who'd been attempting to tunnel her way into my aunt's tent the last time I'd seen her.

Aunt Shannon's name had remained suspiciously absent from all the questionings so far, but that didn't preclude her involvement, regardless of whatever she was keeping in her tent. If she and Mum did end up starting a duel in my absence, they could hardly blame me for not stopping them.

Chloe hesitated. "Um... I'm not sure what your mum actually wants you to do here, but there are more letters that need signing."

"Of course there are." I heaved a sigh. "Meanwhile, my cousin is sitting in a cell for a murder she didn't commit, and nobody seems to care but me. I wish I'd asked to see her instead of coming back here, because she's all alone in there."

"You can go there after work, can't you?"

"Mum told me to stay put until sunset," I said. "She wants me to watch the end of the carnival... the closing ceremony."

She dropped her gaze. "I wish I could help."

I put my head down on the desk then hastily lifted it a moment later in case Grandma yanked my chair out from underneath me again. "It'd be worth it if I was able to figure out who's pulling the strings, but nothing adds up. The person who originally had the thorn-killer toxin is claiming she has flu, there's evidence connecting the shifter to the murder but not the flower club, and to top it all off, my aunt seems entirely innocent."

"Your aunt?" she echoed. "She's not a member of the flower club, is she?"

"No, but Crystal claimed to have got the thorn-killer toxin from someone in the coven, and it sure as hell wasn't Mum," I said. "Between that and whatever she's up to at the carnival, I don't trust Aunt Shannon an inch. Neither does

Mum, considering they've nearly started duelling in public at least twice."

Her brows shot up. "Really?"

"Yeah, they had their wands out and everything," I said. "You'd think Mum would be able to have that tent of hers confiscated if she was genuinely concerned, but she's being completely irrational."

"I imagine it's because she's not concerned with what's inside the tent itself."

I jumped when Grandma spoke, not having seen her pop up behind me—unsurprising, given that she was literally as silent as a ghost.

"What does that mean?" When Grandma didn't answer, I turned to Chloe instead. "Is there something that I'm supposed to be aware of that nobody told me?"

I was curious as to what had driven Mum to break her all-important rule about keeping our public image squeaky clean, yes, but I also needed to fix whatever rift had formed within our family in the past week, and I couldn't do that when I didn't know what had kicked off the fight in the first place.

"Yes, you weren't here the year she created her own raffle," Grandma replied. "She offered a substantial cash prize that turned out to come directly from the coven's funding. Surely someone told you."

"Erm... no." Mum certainly hadn't. In the past five or six years, I'd only been at home for short stretches of time whenever I'd been between jobs, and I certainly hadn't involved myself in the coven's drama during that time. "Aunt Shannon pilfered the coven's funds? How did she get away with that?"

"She didn't," said Chloe, her face flushing a little. "Uh, it wasn't discovered until after the contest. It nearly bank-rupted us."

"Whoa." That would explain Mum's agitation at my aunt's behaviour. "Didn't she put precautions into place to stop Aunt Shannon from trying the same thing again?"

"I imagine she did, yes," Grandma said. "I am no longer involved in discussions of the coven's funding, and good riddance to that."

"And Mum's worried about whatever she's keeping inside that tent of hers?" I surmised. "I guess she could have spent Rowan's inheritance..."

Grandma scoffed. "Do you think she ever planned to leave anything to her youngest daughter, even before she turned her back on her family?"

"Ouch." Poor Rowan. "Then where'd she get the funds? Assuming the tent isn't full of empty boxes."

"Not from her own pockets," said Grandma. "She's a notorious skinflint. One birthday, she bought *me* an empty box."

"She didn't, did she?"

"It was a very pretty box," said my grandmother wist-fully. "I wish I could have brought it with me into the after-world... but it was still rude of her."

I raised an eyebrow at Chloe, who shrugged. "She's right, but your aunt might have dug into her own funds if she wanted to make an impression on the public. If she hasn't already opened that tent of hers, I imagine she's waiting for the closing ceremony. Your mother said you can go and watch."

"It'll probably be too late by then," I pointed out. "I wish Mum had told me herself. Instead, she lectured me for inap-propriate behaviour when she almost started several public fights with her own sister."

"Sometimes, my daughter can't see past her own bias," Grandma said.

I looked at her in surprise, since Grandma almost always took Mum's side in our arguments. "Er... thanks, Grandma."

She gave me a haughty look. "Did you want another magic lesson? Or are you going to make yourself useful and actually get some work done?"

"This counts as work," I said. "Maybe we can come up with ideas as to how Aunt Shannon got her hands on a ton of money. Are you sure she *didn't* pillage the coven's accounts?"

"Positive," said Chloe. "Your mother moved all the coven's bank accounts after that debacle, and I'm not sure anyone but the coven leader can even access most of them."

I'd have to take her word for it on that, because I was no better at handling numbers than I was letters. "What's she doing, then? Selling things on eBay?"

"What on earth is that, a nightclub?" Grandma asked.

"A website you can sell stuff on." The magical world had its equivalent, but while I didn't see my aunt selling any of her valuables, she was resourceful enough to find alternatives. "Legally, mind. Unless she's decided to start dabbling in the magical black market."

"What do you know of the black market?" Grandma scooted over to my desk. "You'd better not have got into any nasty habits while you've been away."

"Don't be absurd." I might have refused to take any of my family's money when I struck out alone, but I drew a line at peddling illegal magical artefacts or dodgy potions. Like that eternally sticky cement Dad had mentioned, or...

Wait a moment.

"She's not selling poisons, is she?" I addressed Grandma, who gave a snort of laughter. "What? It's not impossible."

"She'd have to actually have some skill at brewing them herself."

"Not necessarily." Not if the recipients were greedy enough to shell out cash for a chance at winning the flower contest, anyway. "Or she's buying in bulk and selling at a profit. The possibilities are endless."

Chloe cleared her throat. "If that were the case, there'd be evidence."

"Has anyone actually looked for any?" I asked. "I know you said thorn-killer was tricky to brew, Grandma, except..." I trailed off.

"Except for what?" Grandma said. "Finish your thought. Don't leave it hanging."

I rose to my feet. "Has anyone been in the Henbane Coven's headquarters lately, do you know?"

"What on earth does that have to do with anything?"

"A lot, possibly," I murmured to myself. It was another hunch, but Grandma's earlier mention of the Henbane Coven's gift for brewing poisons came to mind. *They could have made a fortune if they hadn't hoarded them all for their own use...* but what if someone else had swiped the toxin from their headquarters? The remaining members of the coven might have been too busy dealing with the fallout of their leader's arrest to have noticed any break-ins. "Grandma, you said the thorn-killer toxin was the Henbanes' speciality, right?"

"That and a dozen other poisons, yes."

"Their leader was recently arrested," I said slowly. "I can't imagine they've held many meetings since then. There'd have been ample time for someone to sneak into their headquarters and raid their cabinets, wouldn't there?"

"What?" she said sharply. "You think your aunt has been stealing from the Henbanes, do you?"

"You told me yourself that thorn-killer toxin is expensive and difficult to make," I went on. "Not only did the flower club claim to have obtained it from someone in the coven, but Aunt Shannon has also got her hands on a pile of cash that didn't come from the coven's funding. I'd say those two things might be connected."

"Good luck convincing your mother of that one," Grandma said. "Where are you going?"

As I made for the door, Chloe half rose out of her seat. "Wait—you're not going back to the carnival, are you?"

"No, but now's as good a time as any to check up on Aunt Shannon's office," I said. "See if she left any proof behind."

"You most certainly won't," said Grandma.

"Then I'll ask the Henbanes instead," I said to her. "I'm not sure who's running the place these days, but they might not even realise anything is missing unless I ask them."

"You think they'll talk to you?" Grandma scoffed. "After you got their leader arrested?"

Probably not was the honest answer, but this would likely be my only chance to ask some questions while everyone else was at the carnival. I would have bet the Henbanes weren't enjoying the fun like everyone else.

Chloe walked behind me to the door. "I don't think this is a good idea."

"Don't you want to know the truth?" I was far from ready for another confrontation with any of the Henbane witches after the last one I'd seen in person had tried to kill me, but I had no other way to verify that they'd even had any thorn-killer toxin, and it was a mild improvement on breaking into my aunt's office.

I'd save that part for later.

I left Chloe wringing her hands at the door and walked the short distance from the witches' headquarters to the neighbouring building, which held a distinctly neglected air that hadn't been present during my last visit. The Henbanes had never taken as good care of the place as my mother did her own headquarters, but new spiderwebs dusted each window, the curtains were closed, and when I rapped on the door, it was several long minutes before it opened a crack.

"*You,*" hissed a familiar voice.

Ah. "Hello, Leona."

Tiffany Henbane's former apprentice and self-confessed magical dud peered at me through the gap in the door. "If you're here to blame me for your cousin being back in jail, you've come to the wrong place. Go away."

"I didn't come here for that." I might have reminded Leona that she'd once tried to steal my sceptre in an attempt to "cure" her own lack of magical talent—not to mention recruited my cousin to join her coven—and only being underage had spared her a stint in jail herself.

"Then what?" she asked. "You want me to grovel to you and call you Head Witch?"

"No, I want to know if anyone's broken into your store cupboards recently."

She gave a derisive laugh that sounded more like a sob. "Why? What else do you want from us?"

"Is that a yes or a no?" Part of me felt kind of sorry for her. She reminded me of Rowan when she'd been a few years younger, at the mercy of an older and more powerful witch mentor who'd held power over her fate. Evidently, the loss of her leader hadn't driven Leona to leave her coven, but she might not have had anywhere else to go. "I heard your coven specialises in brewing poisons, and there's been one circulating around town that was rumoured to be Tiffany's speciality. Thorn-killer toxin."

"That's what your cousin was accused of," she said

thickly. "Murdering someone with toxin. You're trying to push the blame onto my coven again, aren't you?"

"No, I'm not," I said. "I want to know if any poisons have disappeared from Tiffany's cabinets recently. I'm not trying to trick you. I already *have* a suspect who I think stole them."

Her watery eyes watched me through the gap in the door for a long moment. Then she took in a shaky breath. "I... I thought I was mistaken when I saw, but the thieves took down the wards. If Tiffany was still here, she'd punish me for it, but what does it matter now?"

"Which potions have vanished?" I tried to maintain a calm, almost soothing tone. Leona might be a member of a rival coven who'd tried to kill me, but she was also a kid who'd been left with few options after being born without magic in a town that was pretty much run by it. "I don't necessarily need a list, but it'd help to know if thorn-killer was one of them."

"One of them. Yeah." Her breath rushed out. "I don't think anyone in the coven is using them. It's not us."

"I believe you." I did too. "Thanks for the help."

I might have stayed to ask more questions, but I didn't need to draw attention from the rest of the Henbane Coven, and I still wanted to check up on Aunt Shannon's office while she was at the carnival. Grandma might gripe at me, but if Aunt Shannon had kept any of the poisons she'd obtained from the Henbanes, she'd more likely store them in her office than at her house. She wouldn't risk keeping the toxin anywhere near her own plants.

Back in the witches' headquarters, I made for the stairs. Aunt Shannon's office door was closed and warded, as expected, so I used a detection spell and picked up on a security ward that I easily undid with a wave of my sceptre.

"Robin!" Grandma's ghost popped up behind me. "Don't make me drag you downstairs."

"I'm solving a murder, Grandma."

With another flick of the sceptre, I cast the strongest unlocking charm I could muster. The door burst open, revealing an office almost as messy as mine. Cabinets and shelves filled every inch of space, and a desk sat in the centre, covered in stacks of papers and other junk.

"Your aunt hasn't been brewing poisons, Robin," Grandma said. "Shut the door before she catches you in the act."

"She's too busy at the carnival." I turned to Grandma's ghost. "Leona told me someone *did* recently steal from the Henbanes' storeroom. Now do you believe me?"

Grandma didn't reply, so I returned my attention to the office. Pointing my sceptre at the threshold of the door, I cast a second detection charm and undid another layer of wards before gingerly entering the room. My grandmother laughed unkindly at the awkward dance I had to do to avoid stepping into another magical trap, but I ignored her and undid the ward.

When I reached the desk, my nerves raced with adrenaline, and the letters on the topmost paper on her desk jumped around before my eyes and made it impossible for me to read them. *Think, Robin.* My aunt wouldn't keep incriminating records out in the open, but if she'd handled them recently, the odds of them being in a filing cabinet at the back of the room were low too.

Using my sceptre, I cast an unlocking charm on the desk drawer. A rattling noise responded, and a breeze stirred the papers from Grandma's direction.

"Come to help?" I took a sharp step back when a stack of papers slid to the floor. "I was trying to be subtle, you know."

"She'll know you were the one who undid the wards," Grandma reprimanded me. "Fine, if you're going to persist with this absurdity, let me—"

She cut off with a curse that made me raise my eyebrows in surprise. She'd tried to enter the office, only for her ghostly body to collide with an invisible wall. Aunt Shannon had ghost-proofed her office.

Oh boy.

"The nerve of her!" Grandma raised her arms, and a gust of wind swept into the office with the force of a tidal wave. I gasped in pain as my back slammed into a cabinet while papers flew off the desk and into a swirling dervish.

Catching my balance, I gave another pained yelp when a cabinet door flew open and hit me in the back of the head. Stars twinkled before my eyes, and I hastily dropped to my front to avoid getting hit by another gale-force wind. I crawled underneath the desk, my knees catching on sheets of paper covered in Aunt Shannon's neat handwriting. Pity I couldn't *read* them.

"Grandma, simmer down," I called to her, rubbing the back of my head with my hand. "I'm trying to find proof here, but now you've made a mess of everything."

No response came, but the wind stopped gusting, winning me a few seconds to recover. As I attempted to crawl backwards from under the desk, my head collided with a wooden block.

"Ow." Groaning, I fell onto my side, another throb of pain rippling through my skull. What kind of place was that to put a drawer? A—wait a moment. I lifted my head again, more carefully this time. "Hello, hidden compartment."

One application of my sceptre later, and I unearthed a small pile of papers and a glass bottle that I decided against touching with my bare hands, just in case. I couldn't read all the pages, but the word *poison* leapt out at me, and so did a list of numbers that were clearly prices.

The breeze had died down, so I cautiously rose to my feet. "Grandma, I've got the proof."

She'd vanished. To sulk, no doubt. There was no point in even trying to tidy up behind me, especially as I had the proof of Aunt Shannon's mischief in hand. If I told Mum, she might forgive me for running back to the carnival to warn her... or not.

Calling her would be easier, though I'd need to turn my phone back on and wade through her angry messages from earlier. I reached into my pocket but found my phone wasn't there. Had I dropped it inside Aunt Shannon's office? I peered back into the room but didn't see my phone amid the chaos of open cabinets and scattered papers.

"Robin?" Chloe peered around the corner of the stairs, and her eyes bulged. "What... what happened in there?"

"Grandma happened." After double-checking that my phone wasn't in there, I walked to the stairs. "She got mad at my aunt's anti-ghost protections around her office. Anyway, I have the proof, but I can't find my phone. I'll have to use the landline in my office."

"To call your mother?" asked Chloe. "Erm... the last time I spoke to her, she said she'd blocked your number."

I groaned. "Why? Does she not realise that I might have something important to tell her?"

I returned to my office, part of me expecting to find Grandma on another rampage, but she seemed to have taken her temper tantrum elsewhere in the afterworld. I checked under my desk, but I found no sign of my phone. Come to think of it, I hadn't looked for it since I'd turned the power off to avoid being bombarded by angry voicemail messages from Mum.

"What're you looking for?" Chloe asked. "Your phone? I didn't see you put it down."

"No..." I thought back. "I switched it off back in town, but it might have fallen out of my pocket at some point. At least most people are at the carnival, so it's unlikely to have been stolen."

"Is your brother still out?"

"Yeah." I picked up the landline and called Ramsey's number, but I reached his voicemail instead. "Typical. Tansy's at the carnival, too, and I didn't even have time to find her before Mum sent me packing."

"I'm surprised Tansy didn't find you herself," said Chloe. "Your brother isn't at the police station?"

"No, he was going to talk to the flower club's missing members." Not for the first time, I wished I'd gone with him to Crystal's house instead of coming back to the carnival... though I wouldn't have found proof of my aunt's trickery if I had. "He sent my dad and me back to face my mother's wrath."

"Your dad?" she echoed. "He was at the police station?"

"Yeah, but you know how things are between those two." As my sole co-worker aside from my grandmother's ghost, Chloe had listened to more than one of my rants on my family's ridiculous arguments.

"Where's your dad now?"

"I had to leave him at the carnival," I said. "With luck, he'll still be there to give me moral support when I go to hand Mum proof of her sister's dodgy dealings."

Chloe sucked in a breath. "I'll go with you."

"I don't want you to get in trouble as well." I hoped Mum might think twice about grounding the Head Witch publicly for the second time in a day, but one never really knew.

"Though if Aunt Shannon tries to make a stealthy escape, I might need your help."

"I'll be right behind you."

We left the office, and I kept both eyes open for my missing phone on the way down the road. I'd most likely left it somewhere in the main street, like near the café or the police station. *Of all the timing.* I also scanned the area for Tansy's bright-red tail but with no luck. She must still be digging away behind Aunt Shannon's tent if she hadn't already got inside.

At the end of the woodland path, we joined the carnival's crowd, which seemed to have doubled in size since I'd left. I found myself forced to take a detour around the tents to avoid being trampled by a group of academy students, as the schools must have let their pupils out early to enjoy the fun. I halted behind Aunt Shannon's tent and saw that the spot where Tansy had been digging was deserted, though the churned-up mud formed a hole big enough for a squirrel to fit through.

"Tansy," I called out. "Tansy?"

No reply. Aunt Shannon hadn't caught her, had she? Heart racing, I skirted the tent, only for Aunt Shannon herself to step into my path.

"Aren't you supposed to be back at the office?"

How did *she* know that? Part of me was tempted to whip out the papers I'd found inside her office, but I needed to hand them to Mum first. "My familiar is supposed to be here. Have you seen her?"

"No, I haven't." She took a step closer, eyeing the mud trodden into the back of her tent. "If that's her work, though, I think your mother should know you're here."

"I was going to talk to her anyway." I met her stare. "I unearthed some interesting information concerning the murder, especially concerning the poison used on the victim."

I tried to step around her, but she moved with me, preventing me from walking past her. Now I understood Mum's temptation to hex her and be done with it.

"Robin." Mum's ringing voice cut through the clamour of the crowd. "Get over here now."

Relief warred with wariness and dread. "I would if your sister would be kind enough to step aside."

Aunt Shannon didn't budge, her demeanour statuelike as I edged my way through the gap between her and the tent to where Mum waited, white-lipped with rage. Out of the corner of my eye, I surreptitiously looked for Chloe, but I was on my own. "I came here because I have urgent information for you, but you turned off your phone."

I reached into my pocket for the papers and heard Aunt Shannon move behind me. Swivelling on my heel, I spotted her vanishing from sight around the tent. *Dammit.*

Mum stepped in closer. "Robin, I thought you had more sense than to ignore my warnings, but you've gone too far this time."

"Robin." Dad appeared, breathless, as if he'd come running as soon as he'd heard Mum addressing me. "I wondered where you'd gone."

Ignoring Mum's furious stare on my back, I turned to Dad. "Sorry I left you here, Dad. Have you seen Tansy?"

"No," he said. "Not since before you left. Is something wrong?"

Mum cut him a glare. "I'd advise you to stay out of this."

"Hang on." Alarm flickered in Dad's expression. "Roxanne, Robin wouldn't have defied you if it wasn't important."

I almost expected Mum to hex him, but she simply turned the full force of her coven-leader glare onto him. He took a couple of steps back, his hand creeping towards the pocket where he kept his wand, which he rarely used, but he didn't run.

I seized the chance to step in. "My phone is missing too. Dad, I don't suppose you remember whether I had it with me at the police station?"

"I thought you knew better than to make up stories, Robin," Mum said. "If you *did* lose your phone, Ramsey can return it to you later."

"That's not what I came here for." For the second time, I reached into my pocket for the papers I'd found in Aunt Shannon's office. "Recognise the handwriting on this?"

An instant later, Chloe caught up to us, wild-eyed and gasping apologies. "I'm sorry. I came here with Robin—this was my idea."

"No, it was mine," I said firmly. "Don't punish Chloe for this. I told her to back me up and give you the information."

"What information?" Mum glared at Chloe and then at the papers I'd shoved under her nose. "What is that?"

"I found it in your sister's office," I told her. "It's an inventory of illegal poisons she sold in the past week. Coincidentally, those same poisons recently disappeared from the Henbane Coven's stock."

"You—you broke into my sister's office?" Mum's anger slipped its leash even further. "I didn't realise I needed to put a ward on your office in order for you to obey my orders, but I'll do so if necessary."

Chloe took the paper from me before Mum knocked it out of my hand. "I'm sorry I let Robin leave the office, but that information is incriminating enough that I felt you should know right away. Where's your sister now?"

"Gone," I answered. "She did a runner as soon as she saw me get out that paper. Anyway, I have to say that the figures on that page might explain why another coven member suddenly gained access to a lot of money."

Mum's eyes flashed. "Chloe, tell me everything. Robin, go back to the office at once."

Chloe hurried to her side, but instead of leaving, I returned to my dad. "Sorry about that."

"I can look for your phone," he offered. "Did you have it at the police station?"

"Never mind my phone." I paced towards my aunt's tent. "I need to find my familiar. I think she might have got into Aunt Shannon's tent."

Dad swore under his breath. "She's not here—your aunt isn't, that is. We can go inside—"

"Wait." I held out a hand before he walked into the wards outside the tent. "That place is covered in magical defences, and I haven't had time to remove them all yet."

"I'll fetch your brother," Dad said. "I'm sure Tansy's fine, Robin."

I hesitated. "Are you sure you want to go and see Ramsey alone?"

He inclined his head. "Of course. Besides, I'm your dad."

"And his," I added. "Someday, he'll swallow his pride and admit it."

He merely nodded sadly. "We'll see."

Determination seized me. "I'll go with you."

14

———————

Dad and I left the carnival as fast as we could navigate the crowds that jostled around the stands, seemingly oblivious to the tension circling the flower tent. We escaped to the woodland path and walked to the centre of the town together, swiftly and without speaking. Now might not be the best time for a proper face-to-face reckoning between father and son, but it had waited long enough already.

I led the way to the police station and halted when the automatic doors opened and the shifter from the café walked out.

Dale jumped violently at the sight of me. "Head Witch."

"Er..." What was he doing here? "My brother called you in for questioning again?"

His face flushed. "Uh, yeah... there was a misunderstanding, but I think we've solved it now."

"What misunderstanding?" I asked, figuring there was no point in beating around the bush at this stage. "Does it have to do with why you were back at the café on Saturday after it closed?"

He looked startled. "No. I mean, I did walk past the café again that evening, but I didn't know anyone saw me."

"Then what were you telling the police?"

He fidgeted, lowering his gaze. "Uh... the truth is that I asked Linus out, and he turned me down. Then he asked me out for coffee, but he only wanted to talk about his promotion, and... look, I know what it looks like, but I told your brother I'm not the killer. I don't even know what this plant stuff is."

"Thorn-killer toxin?" What on earth was Ramsey playing at by questioning this guy again? I'd thought he was talking to the flower club members, though he'd admittedly had long enough to pay them both house calls in the time I'd been stuck at my office.

"Yeah. That." He glanced uneasily over his shoulder at the police station doors. "I've never heard of it before. I'm not really a gardening person."

"That's what poisoned Linus," I explained. "Then a bottle of the stuff turned up in my cousin's flat. You can see why I'm taking an interest in anyone who might have been back to the coffee shop on the day of the murder."

"Your cousin lives in there?" he asked. "Really?"

"She lives in the flat above the café." Either he was a much better actor than he appeared, or he'd been oblivious after all, and to be honest, it was more likely to be the latter. "You've never heard of anyone selling thorn-killer toxin? Are you sure?"

The doors slid open for a second time, and Ramsey emerged from the police station. "Robin, why are you here? I thought you were going back to the carnival."

"I have something important to tell you, and you didn't answer the phone," I said. "Speaking of which, I lost mine somewhere around here."

"You lost your phone?" Ramsey's attention fell on my dad and then Dale.

"Sorry, I should go." Dale hastily backed away and fled around the corner.

"What did you say to him?" I asked Ramsey. "That you'd arrest him if you set eyes on him again?"

"No, of course not," he said. "I simply wanted to verify his connection to the victim."

"He mentioned that he asked Linus out but was turned down," I said. "I assume that's what you're referring to."

Dad cleared his throat. "Yes... that's what Jessica told me. I didn't want to pry, but after Rowan was arrested, I had to make things right. For Robin."

There was a long, awkward pause in which he and Ramsey both studiously avoided looking at one another until I spoke. "Ramsey, have you spoken to Crystal yet?"

"Yes." His jaw clenched, his gaze flickering towards Dad. "That can wait until we're back at the carnival. Does our mother know you're here?"

"She's talking to Chloe," I evaded. "I found proof of Aunt Shannon's shady dealings, but Tansy has gone missing, and my phone must have fallen out of my pocket earlier."

"You've lost your familiar *and* your phone?"

"Yes, and our mother decided to help me out by confining me to the office." I paced down the street, looking out for any signs of my missing phone, and turned back to see his face was still set in an expression of incredulity. "I'm telling the truth. Aunt Shannon almost certainly sold the toxin that killed Linus. As for how it got into Rowan's flat..."

"Robin, slow down," he said. "My familiar told me he didn't see anyone break in, and I can verify that."

"Where is Prickles?" asked Dad.

Ramsey pinched his nose between his fingertips. "In my

office. If you really do have something important to share, then come in, both of you."

This wasn't entirely what I'd had in mind, especially since I hadn't even been inside the station at the time during which my phone had disappeared. I had to admit it was vaguely amusing to see the way Ramsey walked stiffly in front of us as if he wanted to tell Dad to leave but didn't quite know how to.

"This place has changed a lot since I last saw it," Dad remarked. "Redecorated, did you?"

"Not me," he said. "I'm not in charge of that."

I bit back a laugh. My brother's office made "spartan" look like an understatement, as Dad saw for himself when my brother beckoned us inside.

Prickles sat next to a neat stack of papers on the desk, though he jumped onto all fours when Dad walked in. "What is *he* doing here?"

Dad couldn't understand the hedgehog's speech, but Prickles's body language was clear enough, and I didn't blame Dad for hovering in the doorway instead of entering the office. "I... well, I really don't have anything else to share, but I want to help Robin."

"Let him stay, Ramsey," I said. To Prickles, I added, "I've narrowed down the window in which the killer planted the evidence in Rowan's room. Are you certain you didn't see anyone go into the café in the time between when the police left and when I came to visit Rowan?"

"I most certainly did not," he said. "What brought this on, exactly?"

"We're close to answers." I turned to Ramsey. "As for what we found out, it turns out that there was a quantity of thorn-killer toxin in the Henbane Coven's headquarters... which has recently been stolen."

"Who told you this?"

"Grandma," I replied. "She made a comment suggesting that thorn-killer toxin is hard to brew and expensive to buy but that the Henbanes specialised in it. Their leader being jailed means they don't have their usual security up, and when I went to ask them, Leona admitted someone stole from the cupboards recently."

Ramsey hissed out a breath. "What exactly connected this to our aunt?"

"I found a list of prices in Aunt Shannon's office," I replied. "If you want to lecture me about breaking into other people's property, you'll have to get in line behind Mum."

"That's not what I—" Ramsey broke off, looking almost as stunned as Dad. "You figured out all that while confined to your office?"

"If you use the term 'confined' loosely," I said. "I'm sure you can ask Tiffany herself to tell you if she had any thorn-killer toxin in her store cupboard, and Rowan would be willing to verify that her mother was aware of the Henbane Coven's talent for brewing poisons."

"You want to speak to our cousin, is that it?"

It hadn't been on my original plan, but maybe I should let Rowan know I was doing my best to get her out of there while I was in the building. "I certainly don't want to talk to Tiffany, but if you do, Rowan's right there, isn't she?"

"Robin." He sighed. "Fine. I'll give you five minutes max."

Dad accompanied us to the jail, presumably not wanting to be left alone in a room with an angry hedgehog.

"Rowan's in here." Ramsey pointed me through a door to the holding cells where the short-term prisoners stayed. "Tiffany is in isolation, so I'll go to see her myself. I can trust you both not to wander off, can't I?"

He ducked out of sight without waiting for an answer, so Dad and I walked towards the holding cells. They were mostly unoccupied except for one.

Rowan sat upright when she saw me approaching. "Hey, Robin."

"Hey," I said. "Sorry I couldn't drop by sooner. I was—"

"At the contest, I know," she said. "I heard your mother won, so I guess that's one less thing to worry about, right?"

"Yeah, but—have you seen my familiar?"

"Tansy?" she echoed. "No, why?"

"Just checking," I said. "I'm in a bit of a tangle. I don't have time to explain everything, but in short: Your mother has been pillaging the Henbane Coven's stores to raise money for her schemes, and Tansy disappeared while she was trying to dig her way into her tent. Oh, and I lost my phone, and we've ruled out pretty much all of the other suspects in the murder."

Her jaw dropped. "Uh... is that all? Robin, I've not even been here a day. And—wait, is your dad back there?"

"He is." I beckoned to him to come forwards, but Dad shook his head. "He doesn't want to get under Ramsey's feet."

She gave a low whistle. "I'm surprised he let you both in here. What's all this about the Henbanes, then?"

"I'm pretty sure your mother broke into their storeroom," I said. "The thorn-killer toxin is hard to brew and expensive to buy, but according to Grandma, the Henbanes were experts. Did your mum know that too?"

"Yeah, she knew." Her brow furrowed. "I always wondered if my mother would take advantage of the power gap after Tiffany was arrested, but I didn't expect her to pillage their stores. It makes sense, though, if the contents were worth a ton of money."

"I have no idea what she actually spent it on," I added. "We'd have to get into the tent first—which is what Tansy was trying to do when she disappeared."

"Yeah, that sounds dodgy," she said. "I don't think my mother would hurt your familiar, though, Robin."

"Still." I shook my head. "I really wanted to get you out of there by now."

"Don't worry about me," she said. "Really, I'm fine. It's Ralph I'm worried about. I hope he's doing okay without me."

Guilt twinged at me. "Sorry. I should have checked up on him."

"Don't feel you have to," she said. "Mal has the key to my flat, and I'm sure he's taking good care of my pets. I wish I could have brought Ralph with me, but I know he wouldn't like being locked up either."

"You won't be in here for long. I'll see to that." Come to think of it, I might as well check up on Ralph while I looked for my phone in the café. It was the least I could do for Rowan.

I scanned the corridor for my dad and spotted him and Ramsey standing near the door, engaged in whispered conversation.

"Whoa." Rowan followed my gaze. "That's a new development. They're talking?"

"I wouldn't speak too soon," I murmured. "Also, I wish it hadn't taken a murder to put them back in touch."

"You never know. This might be a good chance for a fresh start," she said. "Seriously, go and find that familiar of yours and tell her not to run off again."

"I'll be back for you," I promised.

When they noticed my approach, Dad and Ramsey both fell back into awkward silence.

"You're okay?" asked Dad. "Your brother was telling me…"

"Tiffany reluctantly confirmed that she did have thorn-killer toxin inside her headquarters," Ramsey interjected. "I believe our priority should be finding our aunt at once."

"I know, but I promised Rowan I'd check on her familiar on the way back to the carnival," I said. "Also—that might be where I left my phone."

"I'll go with you," Dad offered. "It won't take long."

Ramsey's shoulders tensed, but he inclined his head. "Fine."

After leaving the police station, we walked the short distance to the café. There were even fewer customers than earlier, and only Mal stood behind the counter.

"You're back?" he said. "Listen… I know you're worried about your cousin, but we're a little short-staffed."

"Wasn't Richie in?"

"Went home with a cold, apparently."

I frowned. "All right. I think I might have left my phone here earlier."

"I haven't seen it. Sorry," he said.

"And my familiar?"

"The squirrel? No." He looked mildly confused. "How did you misplace both?"

"Never mind," I said. "Rowan asked me to drop by and check in on her familiar, so I figured I'd look for my phone while I'm here, but I can come back later if it's easier."

"You can take the key and go up there yourself." He reached into his pocket and held out a bundle of keys.

"Oh, thanks." The other keys on the bundle must have belonged to the storeroom and the other rooms in the building, which presumably meant he trusted me not to run off with them. Nice of him.

A nagging doubt prickled at the back of my mind as I went outside and circled the café, where I found the entrance leading to the upper floor. Rowan's flat stood at the top of the stairs, and I had to try several keys before I found one that worked.

The flat was dark and dusty and felt empty without Rowan present. Tansy wasn't there either, but I'd expected as much. When I turned the light on, the dark shape of Ralph the tarantula darted out of sight under the sofa.

"It's just me." I strode across to the living room and crouched down next to him. "Rowan asked me to check on you."

"Is she okay?" he asked in a small voice.

"Yes, she was just worried about you," I said. "I can ask the police if I can take you to visit, but it'll have to be later. I have to go—"

"No." Ralph ran out of the gap under the sofa and climbed up my sleeve. "I can't stay in here alone a moment longer."

"Has anyone else been in here?" I shivered as his furry legs tickled my ears and he ducked inside my collar. "Aside from me?"

"The manager came to check on me last night."

"I meant before then." I walked back across the flat with Ralph hiding behind my hair, conscious that it was usually Tansy who sat in that position. "You were with Rowan when she was cleaning up after the police left on Saturday, right?"

"Yes, I didn't want to leave her alone downstairs," he said. "Her co-worker doesn't like spiders, so I hid out of sight."

"Richie." I paused to lock the door to Rowan's flat behind me. "Say... you didn't see anyone take the keys to the storeroom, did you?"

"I don't know... why?"

"No reason."

I descended the stairs to the lower floor and then ducked back through the main entrance to return the keys to Mal. With that done, I rejoined my brother and father. They weren't talking to one another, but they didn't look quite as uncomfortable as they had earlier either. Progress.

Ramsey eyed the tarantula sitting under my collar. "Why do you have Ralph with you?"

"He doesn't want to stay locked in Rowan's flat," I explained. "Also, my phone isn't in there."

I filled in Ralph on Aunt Shannon's latest schemes as we walked down the high street, though I didn't know if he took any of it in. The noise from the carnival was audible even from the middle of town, and it would keep building until sunset, when the closing ceremony was due to take place. I'd never felt less in the mood for a celebration, though admittedly, I hadn't been present for the year Aunt Shannon had blown most of the coven's money on a raffle. Which reminded me.

"Ramsey," I said hesitantly as we reached the woodland path. "You remember the year when Aunt Shannon decided to organise a raffle that took out most of the coven's budget, don't you?"

"What on earth does that have to do with anything?" he asked.

"Grandma told me it's why Mum and Aunt Shannon are feuding this year," I explained. "It would have been helpful if someone had let me know earlier."

"I assumed you knew," he said. "You would have if you'd been around."

"Would I have actually been helping at the carnival if I was, though? Be realistic."

Who even knew what kind of job I'd have ended up saddled with if I'd stayed here in Wildwood Heath instead of leaving home at eighteen. There weren't exactly a lot of options at hand in a town in which the coven owned practically everything. Most other places of employment were either owned by other covens, who wouldn't employ a Wildwood Witch, or owned by the shifters, who favoured the pack. Really, it was no wonder it had been so hard for Rowan to shake off her mother. Yet Mal had given her a shot, and if someone had tried to ruin it, I wouldn't let them get away with it.

When Ramsey didn't answer, I asked, "Did Crystal actually admit to being in possession of any thorn-killer toxin?"

He glanced briefly at Dad and then said, "No, she denied everything, but someone certainly used the toxin on Ami's flowers."

"Ask Mum if Crystal's name shows up on the list of Aunt Shannon's customers," I told him. "I'll join you as soon as I've found Tansy."

The noise of the carnival soon enveloped us, and I hung back on the woodland path so that I'd stand a better chance of spotting my familiar before I ended up stuck in the middle of the crowd.

"Maybe your familiar will come if you call for her?" Dad suggested.

"I doubt she'll hear me over all this noise."

Ralph climbed onto my shoulder. "I can look for her on the ground if you like."

"I wouldn't advise it. Someone might tread on you."

Rowan's familiar wasn't a fan of crowds, and he withdrew into my collar as we walked into the melee. I lost sight of my brother and dad almost at once, but I managed to duck out of the crowd's path into the gap between Aunt

Shannon's tent and its neighbour. Still no Tansy, but beneath the general noise of the carnival, I could have sworn I heard someone moving around inside the tent. Was that where Aunt Shannon was hiding? Or had Tansy been trapped in there all along?

I circled the tent, prepared to use my sceptre to break in —but I met no resistance at the opening. Instead, I stumbled straight into the tent and found myself facing a maze of boxes. *What in the world?*

At another shuffling noise, I tensed. "Tansy?"

"Robin!" The distant cry raised the hairs on my arms. I broke into a run around the boxes, following the sound.

I'm coming, Tansy.

15

I followed Tansy's squeaks through the maze of boxes that filled the tent, the part of me not consumed with worry for my familiar wondering whether Aunt Shannon had changed her strategy upon the revelation of her dodgy dealings. I'd kind of hoped to return here to find her being arrested, but Tansy's distress drove a spike of panic into me and made it impossible to focus on anything else.

"Tansy," I called out again.

A piteous cry answered, and I heard the shuffle of footsteps a moment before someone collided with me, tackling me with such force that I crashed into a pile of boxes. Dazed and breathless, it took me a moment to realise the sceptre had flown from my grip. This was the third time in a day I'd hit my head, and it seemed to take an age for me to find the familiar glow... below Richie, who stood with his foot resting on top of the sceptre.

"Give that here." I trod closer, and he lifted his hand, revealing that he held my struggling familiar in his grip. "Tansy! Put her down."

"I'm not hurting her," he said. "I wanted you to come here, that's all. Alone."

"This is my aunt's tent." *You don't say, Robin.* Ow, my head hurt.

"She isn't here."

"She isn't?" If Aunt Shannon wasn't here, who had undone the spells on the tent that prevented anyone from getting in?

"No." He adjusted his grip on a squirming Tansy. "The coven hauled her in for questioning. Wanted to know how she paid for all this or something."

They caught her. Good. Mum or Chloe had managed to corner my aunt, but they'd left the tent unattended in the process. What was this guy doing in here, though?

"Let go of her," I warned as Tansy gave another frantic wriggle. He might be small for a shifter, but he was still a lot bigger than Tansy, and he had my sceptre. Not that he could even use it, but his actions screamed desperation and panic, which meant I didn't know what to expect.

"Not yet." He was breathing hard. "I want you to know, Head Witch... I never meant for any of this to happen."

"You killed Linus, didn't you?"

"I didn't—he wasn't supposed to die," he said quietly. "I thought—I thought if Rowan was blamed for poisoning him, she'd get fired."

"You poisoned someone and didn't expect him to die?" I said incredulously. "You took the toxin from the flower club witches, didn't you?"

He grimaced. "Yeah. I only meant to put in a drop or two, but one of those witches showed up at the counter and nearly caught me in the act."

"Araminta," Tansy squeaked from his hand, but of course, he didn't understand her. *Did she see him?* Araminta hadn't even been present for that conversation, but I should have known better than to think she'd be unaware of illicit activity taking place in her own organisation. She certainly hadn't spared any sympathy for Ami.

"Why on earth did you want Rowan gone that badly, though?" Even if the murder had been accidental, he must have harboured a serious grudge to resort to poisoning a customer to get his co-worker fired.

"Because everything... it's all changed since she started working at the café." He spoke fast, his cheeks flushed. "I tried to give her a chance, like Mal did, but we've gone from being the one shifter-owned café in town to just another place that belongs to the coven. Those witches would never have used it as their meeting place before she joined up."

"You're annoyed because you're getting more business?" I raised a brow. "You seriously have your priorities in the wrong order."

"You saw for yourself how they treat the staff," he mumbled. "We have familiars wandering in and out all the time and coven members lurking outside when they think we aren't looking—"

"You mean Rowan's mother?" I guessed. "You know Rowan herself doesn't want her showing up and spying on her either, don't you?"

He shook his head. "It doesn't matter what she wants. Your coven rules the town, and she's part of it whether she likes it or not."

"I beg to differ." I had zero sympathy, not now that he'd revealed the lengths he'd gone to in order to get rid of someone who'd been trying to escape that very coven herself. "Rowan is in prison, taking the blame for a crime you committed, and I don't think you have any intention of confessing, do you?"

No, he'd wanted me alone for a reason, and he'd already disarmed me. *I have to get Tansy away from him first. The sceptre can wait.*

Movement underneath my collar tickled my neck. I'd forgotten I'd brought Rowan's familiar... and Richie was terrified of spiders.

"Ralph," I whispered. "Can you scare him?"

Richie jumped when the tarantula emerged from my collar and crawled down my arm. "What—get that thing away from me!"

"I'm not a thing," Ralph said indignantly.

As Richie backed away, Tansy shot from his hand like a fluffy bullet, hurtled across the tent floor, and scurried up my leg. While Ralph waved his legs threateningly, my gaze landed on the sceptre, which the shifter was no longer standing on. Now was my chance.

I lunged for the sceptre, and Richie shifted into a wolf. In place of the skinny human was a giant shaggy beast covered in grey fur. He was bigger than I'd have expected, though I was used to Jessica's kids, who were more like cuddly puppies when they shifted. This guy's teeth looked sharp enough to rip me open with ease. Now I was in trouble. Nobody in their right mind wanted to face a panicking werewolf in a confined space, and the throbbing pain in the back of my head reminded me he'd done me one injury already.

I reached into my pocket for my wand, and the werewolf leapt at me. Ralph and Tansy both vanished up my sleeves as I crashed into another pile of boxes, which set off another ringing sensation in my skull. I flailed in a nest of cardboard, rolling to the side as the werewolf's claws swiped at the spot where I'd been a moment before.

As I came upright, I found one of the boxes had been

ripped open, revealing a big pink-and-white horse with a horn sticking out of its skull. Unless I'd hit my head harder than I'd thought, it looked as though my aunt had purchased a giant mechanical unicorn. It resembled the one outside the tents designed for small children to ride on. *That* was what Aunt Shannon had been so desperate to hide?

The werewolf lunged for a second time, and I ducked underneath the mechanical unicorn, which came to life with a braying noise followed by cutesy music. The racket startled the werewolf and gave me the chance to duck out of sight behind another box while I figured out what the hell to do. Richie must have known someone would realise he was in here sooner or later, but the sheer volume of noise from outside and the various distractions in the flower tent might prevent anyone from coming to investigate until it was too late. I'd be dead one way or another if those claws or teeth sank into me.

I grabbed my wand and fired a freeze-frame spell at the werewolf, which missed and hit the mechanical unicorn instead. The music and movement stopped, and the werewolf stalked towards me, no longer distracted by the noise. *Argh.*

I cast another spell, which flew over the werewolf's shoulder. With boxes blocking most escape routes, I had no chance but to run in a straight line and around a corner. If he'd been able to speak, he might have mocked me for retreating, but I had zero desire to be torn to shreds for standing my ground against a rampaging werewolf, especially without my sceptre.

I ran full tilt, the werewolf's feet pounding against the tent floor and ripping holes in the fabric as he easily gained on me. I found myself wishing I'd taken up a regular running habit since I'd moved back home, though even the most athletic human didn't stand a chance of outrunning a rampaging shifter. Worse, I'd lost sight of the sceptre, and thanks to the werewolf's teeth snapping at my heels, I could only run forward, not back. Boxes crashed left and right, and while I glimpsed Tansy's fluffy red tail as she darted about, trying to distract the werewolf, I was more worried about him catching her than me.

I veered around a corner and cast yet another freeze-frame spell, this one hitting its target and winning me a little time. I jogged on past another row of boxes, breathing hard. I couldn't keep up this pace forever, but there were few places to hide. Thanks to my aunt's commitment to secrecy, I hadn't a clue what else was in those boxes... but then again, neither did Richie.

Here goes nothing. I cast an opening charm on one of the boxes directly in the werewolf's path. The box sprang open like a jack-in-the-box, and a giant slot machine emerged. The werewolf hissed in anger as the machine began playing loud, garish music. Okay, I could work with that.

As the werewolf shook off the freeze-frame spell, I began to run again, flinging spells over my shoulder at the boxes without turning back to see what kind of madness I'd left in my wake. Given the racket that exploded against my eardrums, Aunt Shannon had set up an entire amusement arcade in here. The assault on the werewolf's enhanced senses must have been driving him out of his mind. *More's the pity.*

A familiar glow filled the tent, emanating from a spot in front of me. The sceptre. I must be close, and sure enough, I rounded yet another corner and spotted a familiar mechanical unicorn.

"Here!" Tansy squeaked, trying unsuccessfully to lift the sceptre into the air.

I ran to her side and gasped out a thanks. As I grabbed the sceptre, Ralph emerged from my sleeve and swiftly withdrew. "What *is* that?"

I turned, finally taking in the full extent of my aunt's handiwork. A giant carousel dominated the centre of the tent, surrounded by various arcade games and even a bouncy castle. The werewolf was somewhere in there, but I must have run faster than I'd thought, or else he'd got himself lost in the maze of brightness and sound.

I raised the sceptre—and my dad and brother came running into the tent. Both stared at the scene in front of us in bewilderment.

"What...?" Ramsey swivelled towards me. "What is this?"

"Hey," I said breathlessly. "There's a rampaging werewolf on the loose in here, who also happens to be the murderer you're looking for. Want to help me draw him out?"

Without waiting for an answer, I lifted the sceptre and cast the most powerful revealing spell I could muster. Light flared from the sceptre, dazzling my eyes, and the entire tent flew into the air, exposing my aunt's mad plans for the world to see.

The werewolf came staggering into view, blinking in the blinding lights, and I cast a freeze-frame spell. As his body froze on the spot, Tansy leapt forward and climbed onto his head.

"Come and get him," she called.

Recovering from his shock, my brother advanced on the werewolf, pulling out a pair of handcuffs. "He's the killer? Are you sure?"

"I'm sure," I said. "Richie's a barista at the café, and he killed Linus by accident when he was trying to get Rowan fired. He'll confess if you get him back into his human form."

"Grab the fur behind his ears," Dad said suddenly. "That tends to make a werewolf uncomfortable enough to shift back into a human."

"It does?" Ramsey gave him a bewildered look, though it made sense for Dad to know, given his experience chasing around a pair of rambunctious werewolf kids. This guy was a fully grown wolf, but the same principle applied.

It was then that I noticed my mother watching us... along with everyone else who'd been in the flower-contest tent. *Here we go.*

"What is going on?" Mum demanded, but Ramsey was too busy wrestling a pair of handcuffs onto the werewolf to answer.

Dad moved in to explain it to her. I had to admit, I hadn't expected the two of them to have another civil conversation at all in my lifetime, let alone one in such a bizarre setting. The growing crowd prompted Ramsey to order his officers to take Richie away without him shifting back into a human first, but the attendants of the carnival seemed more interested in the contents of my aunt's tent than the arrest taking place right in front of their eyes.

I spotted Aunt Shannon near the back of the crowd, her manner uncharacteristically subdued. She didn't even look annoyed at the mess I'd made of her tent, though she doubtless had bigger problems to worry about.

"She really worked hard on this," I said to Mum. "Pity it was funded by selling black-market poison. I hope she didn't sell it to anyone else who might use it for nefarious purposes."

"We have the names of everyone on that list you found

in her office," said Mum. "How on earth did you end up in her tent with a murderer, Robin?"

"Richie captured my familiar to lure me in here," I explained. "I'm not sure what he was thinking, taking on the Head Witch alone, but he realised I'd figured out his involvement in Linus's death and panicked. I suppose he figured that you were all too distracted to notice him sneaking around."

"You were lucky," said Dad. "I wish you'd told me before you came after him alone."

"I heard Tansy calling for me and had to get her out." My familiar wrapped her fluffy tail around the back of my neck. Ralph had crawled back into my sleeve, hiding from all the attention. "At a guess, he caught Tansy behind the tent and seized on his chance. I'm not sure how he undid all the spells Aunt Shannon used to prevent anyone from breaking in..."

"He didn't," Mum said quietly. "I did. Your aunt raised such a song and dance with the council that it took all our efforts to calm her down, and he must have sneaked in there when our backs were turned. I'm sorry."

"It's not your fault." Man, this was turning into a weird day. I didn't think I'd ever seen my mother look that remorseful in my life. "It's hers."

"I should still have exposed this sooner." She gestured at the tent, which lay in bright-yellow folds around its contents. "I should also have guessed that she'd have gone after the Henbanes' supplies. She must have had her eye on them from the moment of Tiffany's arrest."

"Yeah." I doubted she'd have cared that her business venture had ended in someone's death. "Ah—did you find out what went on with the flower club? Who actually killed Ami's plants?"

"That I don't know, but I can guess," she said. "The same person who Richie took the toxin from."

Crystal, then. I looked for Ramsey, who held out my phone. "Is this yours, Robin? I found it in the clothes Richie left behind when he shifted."

"*He* took my phone." I reached out a hand to take it back. "I suppose he figured out I was close to guessing the truth when I saw him at the café, and he wanted to make it harder for me to tell anyone."

"He didn't count on you having so many of us willing to help you." Dad hugged me. "I'm glad you're okay, Robin."

Mum cleared her throat. "The Head Witch and I have to discuss how to proceed with the carnival and what to do with the contents of Shannon's tent."

"Of course." Dad stepped back and gave me a smile, and I walked with Mum towards the flower tent. The police were trying to keep people away from Aunt Shannon's tent, but as it now lay open for the world to see, they weren't having much luck. Excited children were already starting to play on the carousel and in the bouncy castle.

"What's going to happen to her?" I indicated Aunt Shannon, who remained lurking near the back of the crowd as if she was trying to look like part of the scenery. "I know she has enough clout within the coven to avoid arrest, but she can't be let off with just a slap on the wrist."

"She'll have to pay back all the money she gained from selling those poisons." Ramsey caught up with us. "The police will search her house and office extensively. We'll leave no stone unturned. And her daughter will be released immediately, of course."

"Good," I said firmly. "What about her other daughter? I wouldn't be surprised if she had Vanessa do the actual stealing herself."

"We'll see what we can unearth," he said. "Now—the carnival. Mother, do you still want the fireworks display to go ahead as scheduled? One arrest won't take all my officers away, but I know this turn of events has upended our plans."

Mum looked at me, to my surprise. "That should be up to the Head Witch, I think."

My mouth parted. "I'm more concerned with how you're going to get rid of that expensive gear of Aunt Shannon's. It's a bit late to put the unicorn back into the box."

"You think we should get rid of it?"

Since when was I the one to make the final call? "No. I mean, those kids are already having fun playing on the bouncy castle, and it'll put a damper on the event if we confiscate the whole lot when everyone already knows it's there. If anything, it's a handy distraction."

It was lucky my fight with the werewolf hadn't made a complete mess of the place, and I had no problem letting our visitors play with Aunt Shannon's toys. If she ended up in a financial hole as a result, all the better.

"If you say so, Head Witch," said Mum. "And the fireworks?"

"They can go ahead, too, and please don't call me that," I said. "If you want to make up for putting me under house arrest, a simple 'sorry' would do."

Mum's mouth thinned, and I wished I hadn't said anything, but I was too tired for word games. In truth, I felt more like getting an early night than watching the fireworks display.

"Very well, Robin," she said. "I understand if you don't want to attend the ceremony, but we need to decide whether to reference the flower contest at all. With the second-prize winner implicated in illegal activities and the third possibly linked to cheating..."

"I think it was probably Crystal who used the toxin, and Araminta just overlooked the rule-breaking in front of her own eyes," I said. "Though I don't think we need to give Aunt Shannon the chance to redeem herself by mentioning she bought all this. You should get up there alone and take credit."

"Agreed," Ramsey said to my surprise. "Claim that it was the coven's work. Your sister won't intervene if I invite her to the police station during the ceremony."

"Excellent." I grinned. "Wait, does that mean you aren't going to be there?"

"I never intended to stay," he said. "Not unless I was still on duty."

"Figures." Taking the night off was a foreign concept to him. Still, at least it meant Aunt Shannon wouldn't be around either. "If you change your mind, Dad and I will still be here."

Before he could respond, a passing coven member flagged down Mum to ask what was going on. While she and Ramsey explained, I returned to my dad—and did a double take when I saw Harvey standing beside him.

"Oh, hey, Harvey," I said. "Dad, this isn't how I planned to introduce the two of you."

"I expected not, but I'm glad you're okay."

Harvey pulled me into a hug. "So am I. I can't believe you started a fight with a werewolf."

"Believe me, I didn't start the fight," I told him. "He was panicking, I think. I set Rowan's familiar on him, and he's terrified of spiders."

"Shifters can still hurt people when they panic," said Dad. "You were lucky."

"I know." I turned to Harvey. "How much did he tell you?"

"Enough to know I should have been here from the start," he said. "I should congratulate your mum on winning the flower contest too."

"I think she's busy." I looked in her direction and saw her eyes narrow when she saw Dad and Harvey side by side, suggesting she was annoyed that I'd introduced him to my dad before her. Hardly my fault, as I'd offered to introduce them at least once, and she'd declined on the grounds that she had more important things to concern herself with than my love life.

It wasn't entirely surprising when Mum strode over to join us shortly and regarded my boyfriend with a coolly polite expression. "You must be Harvey."

"Yeah... that's me." Harvey extended a hand. "It's nice to officially meet you, Lady Wildwood."

Using her official title was bound to make a good impression, and it was a relief when she accepted the handshake. "I do hope you aren't distracting my daughter from her duties as Head Witch."

"I wouldn't dream of it," he said.

I suppressed an eye-roll. If she hadn't been my mother, I'd have suspected the word "distracting" referred to certain, ahem, activities and not to us seeing one another in general. That was Mum for you, though.

"I take it I'm not on duty tonight, so I can watch the end of the ceremony?" I asked her.

"You do plan to stay?"

Now that Harvey was here, I found my mood had improved tenfold. "Yes. Also, I'm starving, so I'm going to grab something to eat while we wait for Rowan to get out of jail."

Mum's lips compressed, but she nodded. "Yes, I expect she'll be here within the hour."

We didn't have to wait long. Harvey and I bought lunch and were haggling over one of the arcade machines when Rowan tackle-hugged me from behind and dislodged Ralph from my sleeve.

"I'm glad you're okay!" she said to both me and Ralph, who climbed onto her hand and settled on her shoulder.

"Your familiar is the reason we caught the real culprit," I told her. "I don't know how much the police told you…"

"I saw them bring Richie in," she said. "I knew he never liked me, but I'd never have expected anything like that from him."

"He wanted you to get fired, not arrested," I clarified. "Not that that's an excuse. He didn't intend for anyone to die, supposedly, but that's what happens when you mess with dangerous substances. I wish I'd been able to figure it out sooner, but I didn't realise there was only the one set of spare keys for your flat."

"Hey, I didn't work it out, and I *live* there," she pointed out. "Also, I've worked alongside the guy for weeks and didn't peg him for a killer, even an unintentional one."

"He took issue with the witches using the café as their meeting point," I added. "Said the coven was taking over the café like everywhere else."

Her brow wrinkled. "That's not technically wrong, but it's hardly *my* fault my mother won't leave me alone. And those flower club witches are as annoying to me as the rest of us."

"Your mother's off to be questioned by the police herself," I said to her. "She won't be showing her face here again."

"She really went all out on this," she remarked, gesturing to the arcade. "This was all her work?"

"Yep." I told her everything as we explored the arcade and took turns playing the various games with Harvey.

Not long afterwards, the crackle of static from a loudspeaker spell drew everyone's attention, and Mum's voice rang across the crowd. "I have a couple of announcements to make."

Tension gripped me, and when I looked for the source of her voice, I saw that she'd moved the stage from the flower tent so that it now faced the carnival itself from the front.

"Firstly, I'd like to thank you all for attending the carnival, especially those of you who came to the flower contest," she said. "Unfortunately, we found several cases of behind-the-scenes sabotage which rendered the results unfairly unbalanced."

A murmur arose, mostly of surprise, and the crowd waited for her to continue—including me. *What is she doing?*

"The results of the flower contest are nullified," she went on, "and instead, I'll be handing my trophy to Ami, who was the unfortunate victim of this sabotage. As an experienced member of the flower club and a previous entrant, I have no doubt she is deserving of the prize."

More surprise rippled through the crowd, followed by applause. I clapped, too, though I was surprised that she'd hand over the trophy so readily. She'd won every year except when *her* mother had been the main contender, so it wouldn't be a big sacrifice for her, but it was refreshing to say the least.

As I looked for Ami, I caught sight of Araminta standing at the flower tent, her expression incensed. I couldn't summon up much sympathy for her. Even if she hadn't cheated after all, she'd been looking out for herself alone, and it was her indifferent leadership that Aunt Shannon had exploited when she'd handed the toxin over to Crystal.

The conflict between us wasn't over, I was sure, but for once in my life, I had the rest of the day free, and I fully intended to make the most of my dad, Harvey, *and* Rowan being in the same place. Not to mention Mum and Ramsey. Yes, certain members of our group couldn't interact with one another without sustained awkwardness, but I couldn't have it all.

"That's everything," Mum finished. "I hope you enjoy the rest of the day."

Fireworks exploded across the sky, ending her speech, and I stood back with the rest of the crowd to enjoy the show.

ABOUT THE AUTHOR

Elle Adams lives in the middle of England, where she spends most of her time reading an ever-growing mountain of books, planning her next adventure, or writing. Elle's books are humorous mysteries with a paranormal twist, packed with magical mayhem.

She also writes urban and contemporary fantasy novels as Emma L. Adams.

Visit http://www.elleadamsauthor.com/ to find out more about Elle's books, or sign up to her newsletter at: smarturl.it/ElleAdamsNewsletter

9 781915 250414